The Silent Sufferer

Written by

Frank Negolfka

CHAPTER 1 *The Catalyst*

It's December 13, 1998. My father sits upstairs alone in his bedroom. In one hand, he has a phone; the other hand is clenching a sawed off shotgun. My dad is in the middle of a mental breakdown. He is threatening to take his own life and he is talking to a crisis negotiator.

My mom was in the house with him when this crisis started. He told her this was the end; that he was going to kill himself. He demanded that she leave the house. She had two kids and no clue what he was capable of doing at this point. She had no choice but to go.

I was on my way home from playing indoor basketball with my cousin and his friends. We took a left to head down the street leading to my house, I saw several cop cars parked in front of my house. Why would they be at my house?

As we pulled closer, an officer approached the car. "Sorry fellas, can't go down this way."

"Why not?" my cousin asked.

The officer replied, "Some nut job has a gun and is threatening to shoot himself."

"In that house?" I asked, pointing to my house.

"Yep," he replied.

I jumped out and started walking towards the house. Several officers ran towards me and told me I wasn't allowed to be there. I wasn't allowed? This is my house!

"The man inside has a gun and we're just trying to keep everyone safe." The cops escorted us to the corner of the street, about 200 feet away from my house. There was already a small crowd gathered there. They huddled on the corner, waiting to see what was going to happen next. They seemed excited by what was going on. I could hear them asking, "will he do it?" It almost seemed like they wanted him to…

Once my mom was able to verify that I was her son, I was able to go and join her. I was glad to be away from those people. I don't know how much longer I would have been able to listen before I snapped at them.

As time went on, more and more cops started to arrive. From what I was able to gather, this must have meant that his threats were getting more severe.

I was unaware of the extent of the mental health problems my dad suffered from. I was only fourteen at the time and that's not something you give your child all the details to. This wasn't his first attempt to take his life. This was, however, the first time he brought a gun into his plan. My dad had gotten a DUI earlier that week. I guess that was the final straw.

We asked if there was anything they could tell us, any kind of updates. They told us the negotiator said they were talking about fishing and they called his buddy Ralph. Ralph was on his way.

My dad loved fishing. That was one of the few topics you could talk about that would distract him. He must have been telling this guy stories about his fishing trips with Ralph. Ralph was a friend of my dad's. They met while working at Hopkins International Airport. We were close with Ralph's family and would do things with them on occasion.

When my dad and Ralph got together, they were like an old Saturday Night Live skit. They would talk in weird accents and were constantly joking around. Ralph was one of the few people who could bring out that happiness in my dad. When he was like that, I loved being around him.

I figured once Ralph got there, everything would be alright. He'd walk out the door and this would be something we would all laugh about one day.

At the time, I didn't realize how serious this really was. The reality had not clicked. That was until the swat team arrived. They pulled up in a giant armored vehicle. There were at least eight of them. These guys were the real deal. They made the local cops look like rookies.

Ralph arrived about an hour later. He lived pretty far away, so he must have driven really fast to get there. He had a big blue conversion van. They allowed him to park it in front of the house. We all got into the van. Ralph hit us with a joke before we could even get in. He did a great job to alleviate the tension.

We all just sat in the van. Ralph turned on the oldies station. "We might as well have fun while we wait," he said in a goofy voice. We all laughed.

We sat in the van for an hour. No one talked to us. No one told us anything. I wondered why they didn't just let Ralph go in and get this whole thing over with. That wasn't even an option to them.

I could see the SWAT team getting ready for something.They were covered in bulletproof materials. They had helmets and shields. They were strapping up. I thought this was overkill. My dad wasn't going to hurt anyone.

I watched them as they approached the house slowly and with extreme caution. I was confused as to why they were trying to enter the house. Why did they need so many people? All I could do was watch from the backseat of the van.

There were four of them that entered the house. They acted as if they were prepared for war. Every step and movement was tactical. I could no longer see any of them.

After only a few minutes, the swat team walked out of the house. This time, though, they weren't cautious. They walked out very nonchalantly. They had their shields down and were taking their helmets off. That was when I realized he had done it.

I never heard the shot that took my father's life.

I would have liked to know what went through his mind in his final minutes. I never got the chance to try to help or even to say goodbye. That night would leave me with a lot of unanswered questions. That night would serve as the catalyst for the rest of my life.

CHAPTER 2 *On the Field*

Let's rewind. I want to go back to before that night. I want to go back to the summer of 98. Two weeks before my freshman year began. I was a football player and it was our first day of practice. There I stood, this chubby, handsome, chili-bowl haircut sporting badass. I was so nervous at this point in my life. I was only slightly outgoing and being around a bunch of people I didn't know wasn't the most comfortable for me.

We all stood around making small talk. Some of us had played together in the past, but we were unaware of what we were really getting into.

The area where we had practice was basically two football fields next to each other. One was for the freshman team and the other was for the junior varsity and varsity teams. Varsity and J.V. were already practicing as we waited for our practice to begin.

Varsity must have taken a water break because before we knew it, there were four senior guys walking toward us and instantly started to insult each kid on the freshmen team.

The leader of the pack was a tall, skinny, black kid who berated us with the comedic timing of Don Rickles. His first target was the nicest kid on the planet; a real gentle soul. He told him he needed to "tuck his lips in" and that he looked like Bubba from Forrest Gump if he had sickle cell.

The senior guys all laughed and mocked us. What could we do? We were just a bunch of soft kids and these guys looked like grown men to us.

They made their way to me and I was not ready. My last name is Negolfka. We had to write our names and put them on the front of our helmets. I stood there and waited for fat jokes; I was used to them. I knew how to react to fat jokes and even had some comebacks in my pocket for certain jokes but what he said next caught me so off guard, I'll never forget it.

The leader of the pack looked at my helmet, staring at it with a confused look, and asked "What the fuck is your last name?"

"What?" I was genuinely confused why he was upset about my last name.

He repeated, "How the fuck do you say your last name?" He wasn't very happy and I couldn't figure out why he was so irate.

I finally mustered up the courage to whimper out, "Negolfka, my name is Negolfka."

"That shit says n***a fucka."

I had never heard this before and had no clue how to react. If I defended myself, I thought they'd think I was racist.

Just then, seemingly out of nowhere, a voice yelled out "Why don't you mother fuckers shut up. I'll beat all your asses." He said it in a half-joking, half-serious tone.

They continued to insult us as they walked away back over to their practice. I'll always wonder if they walked away out of fear or just because they knew that if they were caught messing with the younger kids, the coaches would make them run until they threw up.

The person who told them to shut up looked at me and said, "What's up? Name's Rodney. And that shit most definitely says 'n***a fucka.'"

Then, we all as a team busted out laughing as he ripped the tape off my helmet and I said "My name's Frank." That was the moment we all became comfortable and high school began.

Football is the ultimate team game. There are eleven men. Each one designated with his own responsibility. All players must work in unison to achieve the common goal. When football is played with passion and fundamentals, it is a thing of beauty to behold. One chink in the armor and you can be deprived of glory. Rule number one in football is to identify your weakness. We found one of ours real quick.

We had a kid whose mom must have wanted him to play or something. He managed to stay on the team for a couple days and by this point, coaches had named him 'Giggles' because he was always smiling like someone had just said something funny. He must have smiled one more time than is allowed on the gridiron because it pissed those coaches off.

"Rodney , Frank… I want you boys to introduce Giggles here to football." The coach had Rodney and I line up next to each other with Giggles on the opposite side. "I want you two to take turns showing Mr.Giggles how we play a contact sport. I want you guys to make sure he doesn't smile on my football field ever again."

The whistle blew and Rodney popped Giggles, throwing him back three yards. The whistle blew again and this time I hit him, knocking him back four yards.

Rodney looked at me with a smirk and said, "Oh I see, you think you're better."

I just smiled at him. The whistle blew again. Rodney cocked back and brought more energy and aggression to this hit. He knocked Giggles right on his ass. Once again, the whistle blew and I rocked this poor kid, lifting him off both his feet and slamming him into the ground. This continued for a couple more hits until the coach finally decided to call off the dogs. When we finished, our teammates were debating who won. We didn't care. We just both knew we did what we were supposed to do and that the message was sent.

Football was a lot of fun for me. Football practice was where I began to find my voice and build leadership qualities. Playing a sport that I loved and being able to do it with kids I now considered friends was awesome!

We were a day away from our first game. We had just finished our last practice before the season was to officially start. I remember everyone was laughing and excited to get the show on the road.

As we were putting our pads away, four seniors walked into our locker room. This big, deep voice yelled out "look at all these freshman pussies." His name was Big Dan. He was a 6'4 offensive lineman and he looked like he could have been a lumberjack.

They came looking for a fight. Big Dan continued to call us all names. I think he wanted to establish his dominance and make sure that we were all afraid of him. He didn't need to because we all were and for good reason!

They started to take kids' helmets and throw them around while laughing in our faces. "Y'all ain't gonna do shit," Big Dan berated us.

We had a kid on the team we called Little Kev. He was 5'5 and nothing but skin and bones. He had eyes that poked out like he had just seen something that shocked him.

The seniors decided to team up on him. Kicking his equipment around. They were just waiting for someone to do something. We all just kind of stood there. The locker room became extremely silent.

"That's what I thought," Big Dan said, as he and his cronies surveyed the damage they had done and headed for the door.

Just then, there was a high pitched scream! "Yaaaaahhhhhh!" It was Little Kev. He jumped onto the bench and leaped towards Big Dan, whose back was turned to him. He wrapped his tiny arms around Big Dan's neck and clenched onto him and he wasn't letting go! The smallest kid in the room had the biggest balls.

I stood there for a moment in disbelief. Then, like clockwork, we all decided we had enough and joined in. There were about five of us on Big Dan before he even knew what was happening. Little Kev had a water bottle and was hitting him over the head repeatedly. Rodney and I threw nonstop jabs into his arms and legs.

We had managed to get him to the ground. This only lasted a good 20 seconds, but the damage was done. We had proven that we weren't going to take any shit.

Our coach came in and told those guys to leave or he would let their coach know what they were doing. I'm sure Big Dan would have kicked our coach's ass, but they knew if they got into trouble, they would be forced to run until they threw up. I always considered that to be our first win of the season.

We were a tremendously talented team. We played well together. There weren't any egos. We were just a group of kids who wanted to hit some people harder than we wanted to be hit.

I was making a name for myself on the field. The upper class kids began to take notice of what I was capable of. Then, I got word that they wanted me to play on the junior varsity team. I was honored by the fact that I was being recognized for the hard work I was putting in. I told them I would gladly play, but still wanted to be part of the freshman team. That was probably the first and the last time that they were so accommodating.

The freshman team went on to play for the championship that year. We were a tough, well-disciplined group of kids, but on that day we ran into some tougher, and more disciplined kids. We got crushed! They had our number from the moment that game kicked off and just like that our season was over.

We had a little award ceremony the next week to celebrate our accomplishments. We all dressed up nicely. This was our last time together as a team. Rodney and I would end up winning Co-MVP awards. We worked our asses off and it was nice to receive the praise. There was nobody I would have rather shared that honor with.

Chapter 3 *The Aftermath*

My father had killed himself a week before Christmas break at school. I figured that would be a good time to catch up on the work that I had missed while I was out. I went to school to pick up my stuff on the last day before the break. I had decided to go around 6:30 at night, hoping I could grab my work and get out of there without having to see anyone.

My mom dropped me off and waited in the car as I went inside the building. As I approached the building, this overwhelming fear and anxiousness took over me. I hadn't seen or talked to anybody at this point and was just eager to get in and get the hell out of there.

My locker was about a one minute walk away from the door. I made it safely there and gathered all the shit I had to do. I thought to myself, my dad just killed himself, they could have given me less shit to do.

I headed towards the door. I was 100 feet away from Christmas vacation. I heard a voice yell out my name.

"Hey Frank," a sweet, little innocent voice hollered out.

I turned with curiosity to see who it was and before me stood the prettiest girl in 9th grade.

Her name was Brandy. She had blonde hair and blue eyes. She was just stunning, but she was as cliche as it could get. She was wearing her cheerleading outfit.

She walked up to me with those baby blues and asked, "Where have you been all week?"

There was something inside of me that just wanted to blurt out that my dad had just shot himself. I don't know why, but I wanted her to feel sympathetic towards me. I thought it would make her like me. I had all these weird feelings and emotions in a matter of seconds.

As I prepared myself to spit it out, I was interrupted. Brandy gave me one of those awkward slaps on the bicep and said, "I gotta go, Merry Christmas" and ran down the hall back towards the group of cheerleaders.

While I watched her walk away, I thought to myself, nobody wants to hear that shit. I felt ashamed at what I was about to say to her. I couldn't believe I was going to use this tragic event to try to garner pity. I felt sick to my stomach for even allowing myself to have thoughts like that. I wasn't that type of person.

At that moment, I realized I never wanted anyone to ever feel bad for me. I didn't want to be the kid whose dad shot himself. I had to remove myself from that and find a way to become someone else. I had to learn who Frank Negolfka really was and find a way to define myself.

That was a rather unfulfilling Christmas break. Christmas didn't have the usual spark that year. My dad used to do anything and everything to delay my sister and I from opening our gifts. He would wait until everyone was ready to open gifts and say, "let me go take a shit first" and he would walk upstairs and spend 20 minutes in the bathroom. I always wondered if he was actually going or just sitting there laughing to himself. As many problems as he had, deep down he was a good guy who liked to joke and mess with people.

After using the bathroom, my dad would proceed to come downstairs and make a pot of coffee. Obviously, this was another well-thought-out stall tactic. My mom, being the sweetheart that she was and knowing that I had absolutely no patience, would allow me to open gifts from my stocking. Those were always some cheap knick-knacks, or deodorant, but like methadone to a junkie, it helped.

My dad would grab his cup of coffee, sit down and it was game time; or so I thought. He would then say, "after this cigarette, we can open gifts." He was a showman. The anticipation did tend to make the whole process better. The thing I liked the most though was that he would wait to open his gifts until everyone else was done.

He wasn't picky. The more obscure the gift was, the more he liked it. If the gift made him laugh, then you did it right and got him a great gift. The best gift he ever got was an Adam Sandler cassette called *What the Hell Happened to Me?* We would drive and listen to it over and over and over. I loved it.

The day had come... My Christmas break had ended and I had no choice but to go back to school. I dreaded the thought of it for the last three weeks. The thought of having to explain myself frightened the shit out of me.

I was sitting in my homeroom. My buddy Nick and I were talking and this girl, Jennifer, joined in the conversation. I felt normal. We were laughing and just like that, my mind was clear. I was at peace for the first time since everything went down.

I made it through a couple of periods at school which were all pretty uneventful. I wasn't sure if people didn't know or if they were just afraid to mention it, but I wasn't going to rock the boat.

There are moments in life that you're able to remember all the details of and on that day, two things happened I'll never be able to forget. The fact that these moments happened within a five minute window of each other makes it even more special to me.

The bell rang, putting an end to the fourth period. I was on my way to history class, all the way on the other side of the building. As I strolled through the halls giving dap and having small talk (as much as you could fit in with the five minutes they give you between classes), I came across my buddy Anthony. Anthony and his brother Thomas were identical twins that I grew up with. They were like my best friends. I'd known them since I was 4 years old.

The way that I met Anthony was like something out of a kid's movie. My other friend Zack and I had decided we were going to go for an adventure. We were going to ride our bikes to the end of the street. At four years old, this journey was of epic proportions to us, even though it was three-tenths of a mile, but fuck it! We were rebels!

We were four houses away from our goal. Our finish line was in our sights. We were so close, but, like all adventurers, we were met with adversity.

There stood a six year-old asshole who went by the name Dylan. He blocked the sidewalk, forcing us to stop dead in our tracks. He was holding a big, red Wiffle ball bat.

He stared us down and said, "What are you assholes doing around here?"

I was completely stunned that a child would talk like that. Zack and I tried to explain to him that we were trying to ride our bikes to the end of the street. That only angered the beast. Dylan told us to "turn the fuck around" or else he was going to beat us with his bat.

We turned around and were going to head home when all of a sudden, Dylan was on the ground, crying and screaming like a baby at the top of his lungs. While our backs were turned, Anthony ran up behind him and tackled him to the ground. Dylan ran away and my hero introduced himself.

I thanked him and he said, "Yeah, stay away from that kid. He's an asshole." I learned that day that kids on the other end of the street had foul, sailor-like mouths.

Anthony escorted us to the end of the street. He just so happened to live in the house at the end of the street. He asked if we wanted to come in and see his toys. Zack denied and rode his bike home while I accepted and made a friend for life.

Anthony and Thomas were the only friends that I had who actually knew my dad. While I was walking down the hall that first day back after Christmas break, I could see Anthony from about 100 feet away. We made eye contact. I wasn't sure what to expect or what he would say, but as we approached each other, he was visibly uncomfortable.

I looked at him and he pretended not to see me. He turned his head towards the wall and just walked by me. I was hurt. Why would this guy ignore me? I thought for sure he would have acknowledged it.

At this point in the day, nobody had said anything about my dad. I walked into fifth period and grabbed a seat. This was one of my least favorite classes because I found history to be boring.

While I sat there still upset at what had just taken place moments earlier, I tried to wrap my mind around the fact that this was the way life would be now. The stigma would always cloud me. This is how people would see me going forward. I didn't like the thought of that.

That's when Rodney entered the classroom. The kid had a smile and an energy that was unmatched to anybody that I'd met at this point in life. He was the only reason I could even tolerate that class. Usually he would walk in and crack a joke, flirt with some girl, or even throw some type of compliment to the teacher. He knew how to turn on the charm.

Today was different though. When he walked into that classroom, he had a look of determination on his face. He stared dead at me and it was like no one else was in the room. Rodney headed straight towards me. My desk was on the other side of the room so he had to walk past everyone and I can only imagine what they were thinking. Rodney never walked into class so quiet and nonverbal.

Honestly, since nobody had said much of anything to me all day, I assumed not that many people knew what happened.

Rodney stood right in front of me and just stared at me for what felt like minutes. I could sense that he knew what happened. I was anxious to hear what he was going to say or do.

What he did next was the most impactful moment that I have ever felt on this Earth.

Rodney grabbed me like he was going in for a tackle. The hug that he gave me was like nothing I've ever experienced. I could feel his compassion. He put his soul into that hug.

Rodney whispered in my ear, "I love you. It's gonna be okay."

That simple gesture meant everything to me. One small act of kindness made me feel like everything would be alright. The fact that he did it in front of a classroom full of people and made sure no one heard what he said to me was even more impressive.

I was so choked up. I was holding back everything. I am not the type who likes to show emotions. I don't even remember if I asked the teacher if I could use the bathroom or just walked out, but I was gone. I stood in front of the sink that had a mirror above it. I looked at myself. This little smirk of happiness came over my face and then I absolutely lost it. I cried so hard and it felt amazing. The weight of everything had been lifted off my shoulders. That was the first time that I had felt peace since my dad died.

Eventually, the school day was over. I made it. All the fears I had built up surrounding that day were gone. I couldn't even stay mad at my friend Anthony. I realized that not only was it rough for me having to be in this situation, but it must also be incredibly difficult for the people around me. If the shoe was on the other foot, how would I handle that? Would I have the courage to do what Rodney did? Would I try to ignore it? Would I make it worse by saying too much or saying the wrong thing?

Chapter 4 *Beer, Beer and more Beer*

I grew up in the city of Euclid. It's just east of Cleveland, Ohio. I went to Euclid High School, which was a rather large public school with around 2,000 students. After we ate lunch, there was a large room we would all gather in called the E-room. The "E" stood for entertainment. There was always something going on in the E-room. You could socialize, catch up on school work, get in a fist fight or find so many other activities. The E-room also had an old air hockey table and some arcade games.

I usually sat with a group of friends. We would just hang out and bullshit since you were only given 20 minutes in there. We sat against the wall towards the back of the room. We were a quiet group. We didn't cause problems or do anything exceptionally fun in there.

That was until one day, for some odd reason, I had change in my pocket. It must have been leftover from buying lunch. I looked over at the row of shitty games and felt the urge to play the arcade version of the NES game N.A.R.C. The game was basically a shoot 'em up where you would shoot and arrest drug dealers.

I put a quarter in and was hooked. For the next couple of weeks, I would race to the E-room and start playing. I was infatuated with beating this game. I knew that there was a chance, if I busted my ass and did everything correctly, that I could beat it in the amount of time that I had. Everyday it seemed like I would get closer to the end of my quest.

One day, when I was quarters deep into the game, I felt a hand grab my shoulder and attempt to yank me away from the game.

I naturally assumed it was one of my asshole buddies thinking they were being funny, so I said. "Get the fuck off me".

Then I heard a raspy, thugged out voice say, "I'm gonna fuck you up and you ain't gonna do shit about it."

I turned to see who was fucking with me. I looked straight into the face of evil. Behind me was this guy Donnie. He wasn't the biggest guy in the world, but he was definitely one of the meanest. He was the kid who was in and out of juvie since he started kindergarten. He was somehow labeled a freshman, but was old enough to vote. He had one of those paper-thin mustaches and was shaving his head in 9th grade. Basically, he was the type of person who didn't give a shit about anything.

Why did this asshole pick me? Was it because I was the biggest and it made him feel like he was back in the yard?

This fucking asshole grabbed me by the throat in front of the entire E-room. I could hear the collective gasps as I struggled to decide what my next move should be, when all of a sudden he just let go.

He yelled out, "I'm sorry," and "sometimes I just can't control myself."

I almost felt bad for him after hearing that. Donnie stuck out both arms to say I give up. He leaned closer giving the impression that he wanted a hug. Who was I to deny this psycho?

I stuck out my arms and leaned towards him. His arm launched back and like a bat out of hell, he took a swing at my face. This asshole just punched me in the face. The room went silent. The punch really didn't phase me because I had a monster for a sister who threw grown-man punches, but the embarrassment that I instantly felt was far worse.

I literally just stood there in total amazement. Do I hit him and risk getting in trouble? If I do, will he beat the shit out of me? I felt like whatever I did it was a lose -lose situation.

Donnie flexed at me like he was going to take another swing and I just flinched. He laughed directly into my face as he walked away. He had managed to drain me of all the pride I was building up. I felt worthless. I was too big to get punked.

I went back to my table. My friends all tried to console me. Their words had no effect and unfortunately, the damage was done. I felt like human garbage. I couldn't stop replaying the memory of the whole incident. I stopped playing N.A.R.C for awhile after that and kind of just hid off in the corner with my friends.

Winters in Ohio can tend to get very boring. The cold, usually harsh, weather conditions make it unbearable at times. Thinking of things to do or even just building up the motivation to head out into the world itself becomes a chore. The weather can lead to bad decisions.

My friend Mike and I were having a conversation via typing when he asked, "Any big weekend plans?"

I replied, "Uh dude, there's a foot of snow and it's freezing."

"Who cares? Let's get some hoes and some forties," Mike said.

I assumed he was joking, but he really seemed to keep pressing the idea of getting drunk. We talked a bit more and were able to get a couple people interested in hanging out. I hopped in the shower, got ready, and headed over to our friend Max's.

Max was a year younger than I was. His parents owned a bar and were barely ever home, so it was a great place to go when we wanted to get a group of people together and possibly get into some trouble.

We managed to get a group of four of us. Max, Mike, Hubba Bubba, and I. We sat there for an hour watching T.V. and bullshitting about "chicks we'd bang" knowing damn well that not a single one of them would even touch us.

Mike per usual said, "Grab some forties and get some chicks."

We all laughed for a moment. That was until Max agreed with him. "Sounds like fun," he said.

It didn't take long for Hubba and I to agree with them. "Fuck it! Let's do it," I said. "Let's get wasted."

We headed towards the convenient store that was a little over a half a mile away. That's not a far walk, but when you're battling the wind and snow, it feels like it takes days. The closer we got, the more we all started to question the idea of buying beer.

"How are we going to buy beer?" Hubb asked.

"We don't look old enough," I said.

I could tell Mike had all this figured out. He was quick to say, "We'll be fine. We'll just ask someone to buy it for us." I thought to myself, yeah, right. This won't work. What a waste of time.

As soon as we got to the store, an ederly black man was getting out of his car. Mike ran up to him and with no hesitation and real excitement, asked the man if he would buy us each a 40 ounce. The man looked at Mike, smirked, and began to laugh. He said, "I wish you the best of luck gentleman, but I'll have to pass."

Mike said, "I tried. Who's next?" The three of us looked at each other, all waiting for the other one to step up to the plate.

Hubb said, "Fuck it. I'll ask."

I'd known Hubb since first grade. He was a chubby kid. Hubb was a very nice guy with a bit of a wild side every now and then. Hubb also spoke with a stutter, but his speech impediment kind of picked and choosed when it wanted to be prevalent. One moment you would have zero suspicion that he stuttered and at other times, it was nearly impossible for him to even utter a simple sentence.

The next car to pull in was an old, beat up, red Camero. The windows were up, but you could clearly hear Bad

Company's'"Feel Like Making Love" pumping out of the car. A cloud of smoke poured from the car as the door opened.

Clearly this person was going to buy us beer, we thought. Hubb ran up to the woman who was probably in her late fifties and before he could utter out one word his stutter began to kick in.

He was a foot away from her and he said, "Cccaaaaannn caaa caaa." Hubb struggled to get anything out. This woman looked at him like he was on drugs. He continued to try to ask her to get us beer and all that came out was "bbbbbeee." Hubb put his hand on her shoulder to let her know everything was okay, but she wasn't aware and began to scream. This woman was so freaked out that she swung her purse towards Hubb and screamed for the police as she stormed back to her car and immediately drove away.

The three of us couldn't contain our laughter. Max was on the ground buried in snow and unable breath. I had tears frozen to my cheeks. After several minutes, we were finally able to gather our composure.

"I guess it's my turn," I said hoping maybe Max would step to the plate. He did not.

I walked to the front of the building, standing a couple feet away from the entrance. My heart began to pound. My hands were shaking from the cold and my nerves.

That's when a blue van pulled up. Out stumbled an already visibly drunk mid-thirties, ex-convict-looking fella. I thought to myself, "If this guy won't do it, we should just go home."

As he approached the store, I blurted out, "Uh hey, any chance you wanna grab me a couple forties?"

The convict snarled at me and said, "Yeah man. I gotcha."

I explained that we needed four because we were going to go and get chicks. Even this guy wasn't fooled. I handed him a twenty dollar bill.

"I'm keeping the change." I mean, I wasn't in the position to argue with him.

After about five minutes, he met us on the side of the building. He dropped the plastic bag on the ground. "Have fun and remember to pull out," he said as he walked away .

Success! We each had our own forty. We headed back towards Max's house. He knew his parents weren't home, but he didn't want to risk getting caught boozing. Hubb suggested a park that was a couple minutes out of our way. We all agreed that sounded like our best course of action.

As we huddled together, each holding up our beer, Mike said, "Cheers gentleman." We clanked our bottles and started drinking.

My first thought was...this is gross. I had beers before but these generic, malt liquor forties were not very tasty. Every sip seemed to taste worse than the last. We slugged 'em down slowly but surely.

Max said, "Let's go to my house and find some hoes."

"Yeah!" we all screamed excitedly. As I took my first step, I could feel the alcohol doing its job. We all stumbled a little bit, trying to learn how to walk on drunk legs.

As we stumbled down the street, we were being so obnoxious- yelling and singing as loud as possible. We may have had a little buzz, but we were definitely putting on a show. We were trying to act more drunk than each other.

That night Hubb won. While I staggered to piss on a fire hydrant, he decided to run up to the front of a car and onto the hood. He stomped on the top of that car while screaming out "USA, USA USA." We gathered around the car and screamed out with him, "USA, USA, USA."

I felt invincible! Drinking was awesome. Needless to say, we never pulled any chicks. We went back to Max's house, ate pizza rolls, and eventually, I fell asleep on the couch. Did we know how to party or what?

That next week at school, I couldn't wait to tell people of my experience. I felt the world needed to know that they were missing out on all the fun. I thought about how much more fun school would be if I was drunk here. All I could think about was the weekend when I would be able to consume some sweet, delicious alcohol.

That was a very slow moving school week, but finally it was Friday. The wait was over. The weekend was here. The first thing I did was talk to Max. He told me to stop over after 6:00. When I arrived, I was very unhappy to see that his mom and three siblings were sitting there. The sight of Max and his family sitting in the living room watching T.V. ruined my weekend. I couldn't let them know how disappointed I was so I said my hello's to everyone and sat on the couch.

Max wasn't the brightest kid I knew. I spent twenty minutes giving him death stares and making faces in an attempt to get his attention. Finally, he looked over. I gave him the let's go look and luckily for me, he understood what it meant.

We went downstairs to his bedroom/basement. I said, "I feel like partying tonight. Let's grab some brews."

Max said, "And do what? I don't wanna drink and sit here with my mom." We hit the horn and started making phone calls. We called everyone we knew and had no success.

"I got an idea." Max went into a closet and began searching for something. He ruffled through tons of clothes and old shoes before stumbling onto a yearbook from last year. As dumb as he was, this was a genius move. Girls always put their numbers in your yearbook.

The first one we called was this girl named Missy. She answered the phone like she was waiting for us to call. We told her we were trying to get into some trouble. She said she knew of a party, but couldn't get alcohol and was probably going to lay low. Max had a thing for this girl and knew if he could get her out, he had a chance.

He said, "I have a case of beer and we could all walk over to this party together."

I looked at him and said, "A case? How are we going to pull that off?"

Max grinned as he explained that he helped his mom at the bar this week and took it. I was so proud of him!

We told Missy we would be over in a half hour. Max grabbed a bookbag and transferred the beers into it. This guy could barely read, but when it came to partying, he was revolutionary.

"I got the beers, you gotta carry them." This only seemed fair considering he did all the dirty work.

Missy met us on the corner of her street. She was on the shorter side, but had very pretty eyes. She looked innocent and sweet, but after talking to her briefly, you knew she was trouble. I thought that was sexy.

Missy said that this party was at this kid Danny's house. Max and I did not really know him, but Missy said he wouldn't care. Plus, Max and I were both big guys. We played football and lifted weights. Who would be dumb enough to try to kick us out of a party?

The hike to Danny's was just over two miles, which normally isn't bad, but it being winter and having to carry the beer filled bookbag made the trip slightly harder.

"Let's have a cold one for the walk," I suggested.

We had three beers each while just walking to the party, hiding the cans as each car would drive by. That was basically how much we drank the week prior and we weren't even at the party yet. I could already feel the alcohol kicking in. My body felt warm and tingly.

Missy didn't even knock on the door. We just walked right in. She knew everyone there and was greeted with hugs and kisses. Max and I just stood there as if we were her security guards. As I looked around, I realized that I didn't know anyone there. That made me feel kind of uncomfortable. Nothing a few beers couldn't fix.

Max and I were very competitive. If we opened a beer at the same time, we would both be watching to see who finished it first. We didn't acknowledge this, but we both knew it was taking place.

The music blared through the house. The music consisted mostly of metal and hippie jams. This party had about 25 people. Most of them were stoners and burnouts.

Danny had an older sister. She was there with a few of her friends, but they were mostly upstairs. They were probably in their early twenties.

We were there for about an hour. People were mostly just talking and casually drinking beers. I felt bored. This wasn't how I envisioned parties.

I grabbed two cans out of the bag. I challenged Max to a contest to see who could chug it faster. We drank as fast as we could staring at each other to see who would win. Max did beat me and it was a good thing because when he was done, he took the can, smashed it into his head, and everyone started to cheer. That really got the party going.

We were becoming the life of the party. Everyone wanted to drink with us and I loved it. This was what I thought a party was like. The music got louder. The people got louder.

That's when Danny's sister came down. "Shut the fuck up Danny. If the cops come, you're dead."

I decided it would be a good time to start singing, "Fuck the police. Fuck the police!" as I pumped my fist into the air. The can proceeded to fly out of my hand and hit the floor in front of his sister. Beer spewed out of the can all over her legs and feet. She was not happy.

"Ugh," she cried out, "who the fuck is going to clean this all up?"

I don't know what came over me or what possessed me to do what I did next. I got down on a bended knee. I looked up at her and said, "I will." I grabbed Danny's sister by the foot. I began to lick from the top of her thigh downwards. I kept going until her big toe was in my mouth. She couldn't refrain from smiling. She stuck out her hand to help me off the floor and gave me a peck on the cheek. The balls I had thanks to my good pal beer.

I went to the bookbag to grab yet another beer and they were all gone. Between Max and I, we had ten beers a piece. I felt good. I was definitely buttered, but there was no way the party was going to end.

Luckily, Danny's sister's friend was going on a beer run for everybody. We threw him twenty bucks and said, "Get as much as you can."

He came back 45 minutes later. Max and I had another case of beer in front of us. We continued to smash beers, hit on everyone we could, and get wasted. I easily drank over 20 beers that night. Max and I were party animals. There was no denying it.

Slowly the party began to die down. The music selection was lighter and people were mostly just lounging around. I was laying on the couch enjoying my drunkenness in all of its glory. Missy stood above me and staring at me with those beautiful eyes. I took her hand.and pulled her in to give her a kiss. Just a little peck. She bit her lip and took a deep breath in. I had her right where I wanted her. Wrapping my hands around her hips, I pulled her body closer to mine. With no hesitation, she put one leg over me and began to straddle me. I was so turned on. She leaned in and we began to make out. My hands traveled up her shirt. I was squeezing her boobs like I wanted to take them home with me. Missy was grinding the hell out of me which felt great, but due to the massive amount of beer I had drunk, I had to piss so bad that it was starting to hurt. I didn't want this to stop, but could no longer hold it in.

"Gimme one minute," I said, as I sprung up from the couch and darted for the bathroom.

I got to the bathroom and the door was locked. I knocked several times with no response from the person inside. "Fuck it," I said, as I ran towards the backdoor to go outside to use the bathroom.

The wind was howling and the snow was really piling up. The snow was at least up to my knee. I curled my body as close to the house as possible to prevent the wind from getting my piss all over the place.

I hurried back into the house. I was covered in snow from the one minute I was outside. I dusted myself off and headed back to Missy.

There she was laying on the couch, looking like perfection. Eyes closed, mouth halfway open and snoring like a lumberjack. She was passed out. I did attempt to wake her with a few subtle pokes and nudges, but she refused to budge. I yelled at her! Pulled one of her shoes off. I tried tickling her. It was all for nought. There was no waking her up. Being the gentleman that I was, I threw a blanket over her and headed to go find Max.

We were both wasted! I told him there was no way we could walk home. I pulled the curtain aside to show him just how bad the weather had gotten.

"Fuck! I guess I can call my dad," Max said, as we looked at each other puzzled.

Max's dad was a pretty cool guy. He said he'd be there in 15 minutes and for us to be outside waiting.

We had to sober up. We began moving around and doing stretches we learned from football. Anything we could think of to get the blood flowing. Smacking each other in the face.

I said, "Honestly dude, I feel pretty good." Max agreed and said he felt fine.

Freezing our asses off, we stood on the front porch. The headlights were so bright on his dad's SUV. Max said, "He's here, be cool."

I took a deep breath in and we headed for the car. I made it halfway there when the snow gobbled up my shoe and flung me towards the ground. I fell face first, straight into the snow. Max attempted to help me up. My weight and those Cleveland weather conditions made it impossible for him to get me up. Instead, I pulled Max down with me.

There we were, 500 pounds of drunken assholes covered head to toe in snow, and laughing at the top of our lungs like we'd just been told the world's funniest joke. With teamwork and determination, we managed to get ourselves up and into the car.

"What are you guys? A bunch of pussies who can't handle their drinks?" Max's dad said as we drove off. "I hope you got some pussy at least."

Drunk me, from the backseat said, "I almost did." Max's dad proceeded to call me a gay pussy who couldn't close the deal.

Max stuck up his thumb like he was hitchhiking and exclaimed with great pride "smell my finger." Max told us how he was fingering Danny's sister. He demonstrated for us what he did. He explained that he took his thumb and jammed it in there like it was "my wiener".

His dad looked at him with utter disbelief. His dad said, "Only my idiot for a son could finger a chick and use the wrong fucking finger." He then showed us how to properly do it for future reference.

We got back to Max's and that was that. My first actual party. I never wanted it to end. I loved the feeling of being drunk. I was finally able to let loose without having to worry about consequences. This was the first time since my dad shot himself that I didn't replay that event in my head. I was free from thinking about it. There was no guilt, no trauma. The first time I didn't envision the bullet entering his chest. Alcohol was my new best friend.

Chapter 5 *The Diagnosis*

Ever since I was a kid, I loved competition. I was the type who hated losing more than I liked winning. I thank Anthony and Thomas, the twins, for that. We were always playing some sport or activity that had to have a winner. Even games like kick the can we turned into a sport . We would even bet on it.

That competitive nature left me with a hole when football season was over. I needed something besides lifting weights to occupy my free time after school.

I had an old football coach, Mr. Crosby, a chubby black man with a gap in his teeth and a personality like no other. He was also the only teacher who acknowledged my dad's death. That meant a lot to me .

He was the coach for the indoor track team. He told me that if I threw the shot put, it would help with my football fundamentals. Mr. Crosby sold me by saying it would work on my discipline, footwork, balance, and technique. He knew how to sell me and it most definitely worked.

The next day, I met him in the upstairs gym at the school. There was only a group of five of us, including a kid I played football with, Rob, who I got along with very well. We were the types that could turn anything into a joke. We always found ways to pick on each other or team up to pick on someone else.

Coach Crosby knew that we were all there to stay in shape for other sports. He would make us run for the first thirty minutes of each practice. I hated running and if it wasn't for football, I would spend my whole life trying to avoid it. I wasn't fast at all, but for a husky guy, I did have pretty good endurance.

Throwing the shot put itself wasn't the most fulfilling activity. Throw it, pick it up, throw it again, and repeat, but it was something to keep me in shape. We would also go down to the weightroom and lift after every practice. Rob and I would either have great workouts where we accomplished a lot, or God awful workouts where we would just fuck around the entire time.

I was starting to get better at shot put and I felt like it was all coming together. The footwork and the way your body uses momentum all was starting to feel very natural. The problem was that I was only throwing the shot put as far as Rob, who was 6'1 and 150 lbs. This made no sense. In the weightroom, it was very clear who had the superior strength.

Everytime I would throw the shot put, there was a little pain in my arm. I just assumed that was normal and it was happening to everyone. My arm would get fatigued very fast and the distance on my throws would shrink after each toss.

Then, one day towards the end of practice, I lined myself up, pressed the ball on my neck, and lunged backwards. My body swung and when I went to extend my arm to throw the shot put, there was an excruciating pain in my right bicep. The shot put just fell out of my hand and landed inches away from hitting my foot. I was in such pain but moments later I felt totally fine.

Coach Crosby took me to see the athletic trainer. I stretched out the arm. There was just a little tightness to it. There was a bump on my bicep almost as big as a baseball. She asked how long the bump had been there. I told her I noticed it towards the end of football season. I honestly thought it was a muscle from all my working out, but it was constantly hard to the touch. She handed me a bag of ice and recommended that I go see a doctor and avoid doing anything athletic until someone was able to take a look at it.

My arm felt fine to me. The pain would come and go. I was prepared to deal with it and not think twice, but since they told me I couldn't do anything athletic at school until I was medically cleared, I had no choice but to go and see a doctor.

My mom, my cousin George, and I headed to the local hospital. As a family, we were always able to turn everything into a joke. At this point, even my dad's suicide was something that we could make humorous.

We arrived at this shitty little doctor's office. The jokes were already going; making fun of the magazines, the decor, the way it smelled. I wanted to get in and get out. I never liked being in a hospital or a doctor's office. It made me uneasy for some reason.

After waiting a couple of minutes, the receptionist said we could go to the room. I hopped on the table. I started to get nervous and started thinking about negative outcomes. What if I had to have surgery? What if they had to cut my arm off? My mind always had a slight tendency to think of things from many different angles. It was a blessing and a curse.

The doctor knocked on the door, "Hope everyone's decent," he chuckled as he walked in. I was always a fan of a good corny joke, so this guy was cool in my book. That feeling wouldn't last very long.

He checked all my vitals, used the tongue depressor and whacked me in the knee to check my cat-like reflexes. It almost seemed like he was purposely avoiding the issue. I thought maybe we could just walk out of there and everything would be good.

When he finally got to my arm, he looked worried. He poked and prodded, pushed and pulled, jammed his fingers into the lump and asked if it hurt.

"No," I replied, even though the pain was more than a mild discomfort. The next time he did it, he looked me dead in the eyes while he pushed into it. The grimace on my face must have been a good indicator that there indeed was pain.

The doctor rolled his chair back closer to the door. He looked at all three of us and said, "I don't know what we're dealing with, but it doesn't look good." He explained that he was going to do a biopsy and he would be back in a couple minutes.

As soon as he walked out, I started to insult the guy. Picking on him about his bad breath and his gray, balding hair. The only reason I was doing this was out of fear. I had enough shit I dealt with. I wasn't ready for bad news.

Once again, he knocked on the door and said "I hope everyone is decent." The joke wasn't funny the second time around and this guy wasn't on my good side at the moment.

"This may hurt a little bit," he said as he pulled the biggest needle I have ever seen in my life out from his jacket. I figured maybe he needed a blood sample. I wasn't sure what he was up to. This doctor didn't seem like the most stable person I'd ever met.

The needle had to have been six inches long and thick.

"I'm going to poke you on the count of three," he said as his countdown began. " One, two…" and before I knew it, this cock sucker stabbed the lump in my arm with the needle. He slowly pushed the needle in. Deeper and deeper the needle went into this lump. I didn't think it could get much worse. I figured he had to be done and then this asshole of a doctor decides to spin this needle in a circular motion while it's sticking inside my arm.

His office was awful but it was right on the waters of good ole Lake Erie. I did everything I could to focus on the water and not the agony that I was in. I felt as if this guy heard my jokes and was purposely trying to inflict as much discomfort as possible.

Just when I thought it was over, Dr. Dickface decided to get one last fuck you out of his system and started to pull on the syringe. He was sucking some type of liquid out of the lump. The pain was almost unbearable.

My dad was big into fishing. We had a boat and a lot of my summers were spent on the lake fishing with him. That's all I could focus on because I knew if I saw that needle in my arm, I would either pass out or punch this man in the face.

Finally he pulled it out. I was able to hold back the tears from streaming down my face. That was, without a doubt, the most painful experience I'd ever had.

The doctor took the syringe and left the room. I explained how badly it hurt. George said that it looked painful and showed me how the doctor was moving it around. He showed how erratic it was. That only made me hate this guy even more.

I'm sure by now you know what happened the third time this guy knocked on the door… and no it wasn't funny and yes it made me want to kill him.

Dr. Dickface sat in his rolling chair. Without even having results or any clue what he was talking about, he proceeded to give his clinical diagnosis.

That man looked my mother dead in her face and told her that the lump on my arm was a tumor and that I had cancer. She sat there stone-faced. My mom was the strongest person I knew. George on the other hand lost it. He was crying. I know that really hit home to him because a few months prior he lost his dad to cancer.

I was in disbelief. I walked into the doctor's office just looking for assurance that I could throw a heavy metal ball and was not ready to walk out with a tumor and cancer.

We walked out and headed to our car. All I could feel was anger. I felt if there was a God, he sure did like picking on me. I sat in the car and my mom did her best to try to console me, but there was nothing she or anyone could say to me.

All I could think about was George's dad, my Uncle Larry. We all watched the cancer eat him up and by the end, he was just a shell of himself.The once charismatic joker started to fade away. I didn't want to die like that; slowly dissolving until the end.

When I got home that night, all I could do was cry. I didn't know what else to do. *This was the first time in my life that I had contemplated suicide*. I thought that would be easier. It would be quick and that would be that. I didn't act on those thoughts but they engulfed me. It seemed like that was the only solution my brain could come up with. I was awake all night with nothing but these thoughts.

The next week, I went to a real hospital; University Hospital Case Medical Center in Cleveland, Ohio. I felt more comfortable there than with that whack job on the lake. They seemed to have their shit together and had a more professional atmosphere.

The first doctor I met with was Dr. Abelmen. He was your typical looking Jewish doctor. He was fresh out of medical school and was just taking over the practice. I was the first person that he had seen that had a tumor. He was truly fascinated by it. I could tell right away that he was looking out for me and would do anything to help me. This was a huge upgrade from the last doctor.

Dr. Abelmen explained to my mother and I that this wouldn't be an easy process. He went over a lot of different options. There was chemotherapy, radiation and surgeries. The tumor was the size of a softball if you cut it in half. It was connected to the top part of my bicep and wrapped around the muscle. There was no way to simply just remove it.

I explained to Dr. Abelmen that my main goal was to be able to play football again. That was the most important thing to me, besides my new love of partying, but I couldn't tell my doctor that. He respected that, but warned me to be very cautious with the activities that I chose to do right now. He wanted me to lift less weights with that arm and encouraged more running to keep in shape.

I smiled and joked, "This is all some clever joke to get me to lose weight, nice try." That eased some of the tension in the room.

When dealing with this type of thing nothing is ever easy. One doctor would send me to a specialist, who would send me to another specialist, who would recommend someone less special, but certified. One visit for one thing would turn into an all day ordeal. Between x-rays, MRI's and bloodwork, it never ended. Mentally, it was starting to get to me. Everything hospital related began to cause me stress.

After all the bullshit, Dr. Abelman, my mother and I finally came up with a game-plan. He was going to surgically remove the tumor. Then, when that was done, I would begin doing a low dose chemotherapy treatment.

Dr. Abelmen told me after the surgery, he would be taking the tumor to a conference in Baltimore, Maryland. That kind of made me upset because I thought that I would get to take it home with me and keep it in a jar. Only part of me was joking about this. I really wanted it for some reason.

The surgery was successful. He went in and took it out. I had to stay in the hospital for a couple days after. God bless my mother for having the patience of a saint because I know for a fact that I was a huge baby. Dealing with me had to be a nightmare. I would whine about everything but not to the doctors or nurses, just to her and she would have to deal with it.

She went home one day and I asked if she could smuggle me in something good to eat and run to Blockbuster to get a couple movies just to pass the time. She returned with some chicken nuggets, which made me happy, but did not go to Blockbuster. She decided that she would just grab a couple VHS tapes from home. They were movies I had seen and had no interest in watching again.

During my temper tantrum, I grabbed a copy of the movie "The Perfect Storm" and threw it against the wall, cracking it open and now making it even more unwatchable. She knew I wasn't mad at her. I was just frustrated with the whole situation. My anger and frustration towards hospitals was really starting to blossom.

I only spent two days in the hospital but I swear it felt like a week to me. I was finally home and able to watch some good movies and television. I couldn't go to school or do anything. My arm was wrapped up in a sling.

One whole week I sat there, rotating from couch, to recliner, to bed. Bob Barker, Maury Povich, and Jerry Springer were my new best friends. They were like family to me. This went on for 8 days, until finally I pleaded with my mom to let me leave the house. The doctor was very specific on letting this heal and not doing anything to tear the stitches or stress the arm.

On Saturday nights, we would go cosmic bowling when we could get a ride. This took place in a nicer city with sexier girls. We loved to go there when we could get a ride and get a group of people together. Everyone was going and I promised to behave.

She caved in and dropped me off at the bowling alley. I met up with Mike, Max, Hubb. There were a bunch of people from school. Usually we would bowl one game and then quit. Then, I would run around the place talking to friends, staring at girls that were out of my league and waiting for someone to fight.

That night, I was super careful. I sat down and tried my best to stay away from everyone. I was just so damn happy to not be on the couch, but I did wonder what my buddy Jerry Springer was up to.

I was able to take advantage of my surgery and convince a couple girls that kisses would make me feel better. They were so kind to oblige.

You could always tell when kids were done bowling. When people would get sick of it, they would be ready to get into some mischief. Bowling balls went flying through the air towards the pins. Balls started being thrown across multiple lanes. This would create tension and usually was the cause of a fight or two. I wasn't there for that though. I was on my best behavior.

As the night progressed, there was a rumbling of tensions growing.

We were in the city of Mentor. They did not take kindly to us Euclid folk. They considered us poor and ghetto. We considered them stuck up assholes. There was mutual hatred. They wanted our street cred and we wanted their women.

What we were hearing through the grapevine involved a few older men. Why the fuck grown men were at cosmic bowling and why were they causing problems in the first place? This was all high school kids besides these jokers.

The lights came on. That was the signal that cosmic bowling was over. They wanted everyone the fuck out of there. I made my rounds saying my goodbyes, dapping up all my dudes and hugging all the hunnies.

I had a great time. It was all worth it. I behaved. I didn't put any stress on my arm. People were respectful to my disability. It was a pleasant experience and I was happy.

All we needed now was Max's cool dad to come and get us. Bowling ended at 12:00, but Max told him 12:30 to always give us time in case of any adventures.

"You better tell that bitch to shut up," echoed through the parking lot.

The two older guys who had problems inside were now screaming in each other's faces. The Mentor guy's girlfriend placed herself in the middle, creating a 120 pound barrier between the two. She had to be the cause of all the problems.

She began to put her hands on the man from Euclid. I knew any moment he was going to flip out. She was calling him every name in the book "You faggot, pussy, my boyfriend will whoop your ass!" she screamed, showing off just how classy she was.

The final straw came when she slapped that man directly in his face. "You pussy" were the last words she uttered as she then hocked a loogie in his general direction.

What happened next caused the brawl at cosmic bowling. The Euclid man grabbed that woman by her face, lifting her off her feet and body-slammed her on to the car parked next to them. That's when all hell broke loose.

The two men started exchanging blows and that was when everyone around decided to jump in. Euclid vs. Mentor was taking place right in front of me and all I could do is watch from the sidelines. All in all, there were roughly forty kids throwing punches, bottles, or anything they could get their hands on. In the distance, you could hear the police sirens already. Someone was smart and had anticipated this getting out of control.

Mike and I were about 50 feet from the chaos. He wasn't a fighter. So I was really shocked when he thought it would he a great idea to scream out, "Fuck waste land!" They were a gang in Mentor.

Well you can probably guess what happened next. Not only did one of them hear it, but was actually in it. This was no small guy. He was 6'0, 260 pounds with a shaved head. He stopped what he was doing and took a B-line straight towards Mike.

"What the fuck did you say?" he screamed as he was face to face with Mike. Mike's face was pale white. With no hesitations and zero remorse, this guy cocked back and with all his force punched Mike in his jaw. He was knocked out cold. Mike fell to the pavement like a sack of potatoes.

Everything inside me wanted to stick up for my friend and defend his honor and the honor of my city, but I couldn't move my arm. Doctors orders.

I thought this guy would walk away. Mike was down and there were still people fighting all around. He targeted me next. He saw my arm wrapped in gauze and a sling holding it in place. I assumed he sensed weakness.

"I just layed your boy out. What the fuck you gonna do about it?" he said as a smile of accomplishment took over his face.

I stood tall, put my chin up and said, "If i didn't have the..." and boom his fist connected with my face. I never even saw the punch coming. I, unlike Mike, managed to stay on my feet. I was honestly unphased by his punch. I attributed that to the adrenaline running and my fear of disobeying the doctors orders.

Now that I was aware that this guy didn't care that I was handicapped and he was out for blood, I had no choice but to defend myself. I thought, oh shit my moms gonna be so mad at me.

I could see this asshole cocking back and getting ready to take another swing at me. I had enough time to react to what was coming this time. His punches missed me. I had to fight back. This guy wasn't just going away. My mind went blank. No thoughts. No repercussions. I lunged towards him. My arm flew out of the sling giving me a wider range of motion. My arm went back slightly. I pulled my fist towards my chest . That's when my elbow collided with full force to the front of his face. I knocked that piece of shit out. He laid there on the ground motionless. I didn't have time to admire my handy work. I grabbed Mike and we took off, headed away from the action.I had to get myself out of harm's way. I was extremely lucky that this didn't end up with me in the hospital. I couldn't imagine explaining it to my mother or   Dr. Abelmen.

The ride home was filled with tales of our heroism. We were bad ass mother fuckers now. Even Max's dad who was usually quick to insult us was proud.

"Guess you boys ain't such pussies after all," he said, as well all laughed in agreement.

On the inside, I was so proud of myself. I stood up for myself and I wasn't scared. The old Frank probably would have never taken a swing. I wasn't the toughest kid. I was always afraid that since I was bigger than most kids I would hurt them. I was also afraid I'd get in trouble when I got home.

That next Monday at school, I walked in like nothing had happened. I thought since I was away from the fight nobody saw what I had done. I was wrong. The first person I bumped into at school was a buddy of mine named Bull. He was very quick to give me props for knocking that dude out. He said he saw it in slow motion and when he retold me the story, it made me sound like a superhero.

The word spread like wildfire. That built my ego up a little bit. I, of course, acted like nothing happened and I didn't care, but I liked that people were talking about me. Anything that would get people to not see me as the kid whose dad shot himself was a plus in my eyes.

The next week, I was ready to start the chemotherapy. I was not exactly thrilled considering I was being sent to the Rainbow Babies section of the hospital. I wasn't a baby. I was a beer-chugging, hooter-squeezing, football player.

From the moment I walked into the facility, I felt awkward. The waiting room was like the play area at McDonalds. There were kids running around and screaming. I thought this is almost as unprofessional as Dr. Dickface's office. The children there looked at me like I was an adult and their parents did the same.

"Frank," a nurse called out. I headed towards the office and into my room. I sat on the table waiting for the doctor to come in; swinging my feet around and playing with everything in the room. My mom even had to yell at me. Maybe I did belong here with the babies.

The doctor came in and explained how everything worked. She had a bit of an attitude and I wasn't very fond of her. The doctor came with a nurse who was upbeat, kind, and you could tell she was a good person. I wished she was the doctor.

I had bad veins and whoever was injecting me or taking blood never got it on the first try. My mom and I would always guess. We devised a system that when we would see the person, we would use our fingers to indicate how many attempts it would take. If you stuck your thumb up, that meant that they would not be able to find the vein. If and very rarely they ever got it on the first try, we would do something special for dinner. We spent a lot of time in the hospitals. This was very entertaining for us.

The nurse's name was Maggie. I sized her up and took her kindness for a weakness. I put my hand by my knee and stuck my thumb out. My mom being the optimistic one only stuck up two fingers. Maggie inserted the needle. I was impressed. She found the vein on the first try. I told her how proud I was and that maybe five percent were able to do that.

The chemotherapy entered my veins. There was a distinct smell. I could never describe it or find anything to match it, but it disgusted me. The smell would put knots in my stomach. I would become nauseous instantly. I fucking hated it with a passion. I was on a low dose too so I could only imagine how it felt to do a full dose.

That's when it hit me. Here I was acting like a baby doing low dose chemo. All those little kids in the waiting room had cancer. Chemo was causing them to lose their hair. They were in the hospital fighting for their lives. I became disgusted at myself. I built up this guilt because I wasn't nearly as sick as them. These poor kids and their parents were going through hell. Coming to that realization really fucked me up.

Constantly going to the doctor and being in the hospital really started to give me anxiety and depression. I thought it started when my dad died, but it was the hospitals. I was there so much. Chemo was draining, but seeing those kids play, unaware of what they were going through was gut-wrenching.

Chapter 6 *The Weekend Crew*

By now, I had a lot of people that were friends, but my crew was getting bigger. I added The Geek, Ritchie, A.K., and Western. They fit in just perfectly. We were a group of idiots. I wouldn't have wanted it any other way.

We also ran with a group of girls. The Geek and Western had sexy sisters and I liked when they were around. The girls would also bring friends, who I also thought were sexy. These girls were more than looks. They were my friends.

Western and his sister had very cool parents; Bob and Peg. They were the type of parents who didn't care that we were always over. Peg would make us food and would sometimes let us drink a sip of her Becks. They were just good people. Plus, we could throw parties there. That's why it was my favorite place to be.

Oh, and did I mention… I got my license. This totally opened up a whole new world of possibilities for us. The days of waiting for our parents to pick us up were over or walking miles to get to someone's house. We could go anywhere we wanted, when my mom was nice enough to let me borrow her car.

We had a 1992 white Geo Tracker. My big ass probably looked funny in this tiny car but fuck it, I didn't care. I loved it. I know it took twenty seconds to go from 0 to 60. I would jam as many people as possible into that car and hit the road. Things were slowly getting back to normal by now. I wasn't spending every day at the hospital. I was back to feeling like a teenager for a while.

Once I had the ability to drive, there was no more standing outside of convenient stores hoping someone would hook us up. We took matters into our own hands. Max and I began going to gas stations and stores to find out which ones would sell us beer. We figured what's the worst they can do, say no? We found that almost every store on 185th in Cleveland would sell us beer. We just had to figure out who was cool and who wasn't worth the attempt to try.

Our favorite was "mountain lady". That's what we called her. She was a big gal, built like a lumberjack. She was mean and ornery and kept chew in her mouth at all times, but she sure did have a crush on Max and I. She would light up like the 4th of July when we would walk in. Mountain Lady would not only let us buy beer but she even gave us free snacks. She didn't work often but when she did, it was like Christmas.

The other gas station used to piss me off. There was an old Vietnam vet who worked there. He was a bigger guy with gray hair and a gray beard. He fucking hated me! He refused to sell me beer. He hated that I would buy gas there but for some reason, he loved Max. If we had to go there, Max was the only one he trusted. No matter what, he could get beer. The only problem was this guy wouldn't shut up. Max would have to talk to him for at least ten minutes every time, even if the store was crowded. It drove me nuts.

With this new found talent of being able to purchase alcohol came opportunity. I figured I was buying beer for myself so why not help the less fortunate who didn't look like they were in their thirties in high school. The deal was simple. I would just charge them double for whatever they wanted. These kids were usually the types who always need a ride as well.

At school, there were these two nerdish guys, K.C and Jimmy. They approached my one day in the E-room.

K.C said, "I want beer and I heard you're the man to come to."

He explained they had never drank before and wanted something fun to do over the weekend. He wanted me to give him the rundown on what he should purchase. K.C. wanted to get drunk but not too drunk. That concept was lost on me.

After school, we all hopped into the tracker. The Geek's sister Heather was also joining us. They jumped into the backseat and we took off. As soon as we hit the road, they both started to get cold feet. So me being the jokester that I am had to start fucking with them. I told them since it was still daytime, I could only go to one store.

"We have to go to the hood gas station," trying to scare them a bit.

"That's cool. We go there all the time," K.C said, trying to hide the fact that he was nervous.

Jimmy was wearing a baby blue Nike shirt. "Dude you gotta take that shit off in this neighborhood. I'm not getting shot because of you," I said, looking over at Heather as she tried to hide the smile on her face.

We pulled into the parking lot of the gas station that Mountain Lady worked at. Her truck was parked in its usual spot so I knew we were all good.

"Okay, what do you guys want?" I asked.

"We want a sixer," he said.

This just angered me. I thought to myself... a sixer? I could drink that on the ride home. What a waste of time this was.

"Twenty bucks ladies and the sixer is all yours." They gladly handed me the money.

I walked in and grabbed a six pack of Budweiser. The Mountain Lady was happy to see me. She flirted with me a bit and I hit her with my beautiful smile. I told her I got a buddy in my car that I was fucking with and I was gonna run out of there pretending like I stole something. She laughed and said go for it. I opened the door and ran back to the car screaming, "Fuck! Fuck! Fuck!"

I contemplated jumping across the hood but knew that outcome would not go as planned.

"We're going to jail!" I yelled as I started the car and began to pull off. I looked in the rearview mirror and could see the look of horror on their faces.

As we sped off, my girl Mountain Lady peels open the door and hollers out, "You piece of shit! Don't you ever fucking come back!" I couldn't believe she did that. Bless her soul. I was dying of laughter on the inside.

"I need a beer," I said.

K.C in shock still said, "Help yourself."

I opened the can and began chugging a beer. I explained that some gangbanger tried to take their money from me. I had to kick his ass and steal the beer. It was the best I could come up with. I slammed the beer and asked for another because my nerves were shot.

"Take it," he said. They just wanted more and more details.

By the time I got these guys back to their house, they had two beers left. I drank four beers in seven minutes. These poor kids were left with one beer apiece and it cost them twenty dollars. I forced them to get out of the car by saying I had to hide the car. They left out and I drove off like a demon. Heather and I could not contain our laughter. Everything had worked to perfection.

While we sat there smiling from ear to ear, something hit me. This paralyzing feeling had taken over me. I could see Heather laughing but no sound was coming out. This overwhelming feeling of suicide was all I could think about. In an instant, I began to think I should crash the car. I couldn't overcome this desire to die. I also couldn't justify what was happening in my head. I needed it to stop and it wouldn't. The thoughts were relentless.

That feeling lasted about a minute. I was able to gather myself. Heather had no clue what just took place. I didn't say anything about it. Fuck, I thought it was weird.

Later that weekend, there was a buzz amongst my friends that we were all going to "The Spot." I loved going there. The Spot was a place that was up the hill and in the woods off the freeway. This was a place we could go where there were no rules. Our own little piece of anarchy smack dab in the suburbs. It was our hidden gem.

The Spot was off in the cut. The first step to getting there was to know what street to go down. Very few people even knew the street existed. Then, you would have to drive up or walk a hill that was about a half a mile up. There were a couple of old baseball fields and concession stands hidden up there. You had to venture past those and into the wooded area. This is where you would come across "The Bridge of Death". The bridge was the length of a football field and thirty feet from side to side. The only problem was the bridge was dilapidated. There were holes scattered all around. One false move or wrong step and you would drop fifty feet. You may not have died but the drop was definitely going to ruin your weekend.

Once you navigated the bridge, you would take a left. Three minutes later, you were at The Spot. It was simply a firepit with nothing but trees around. When you were here, the rest of the world didn't exist.

This weekend, we were meeting up there to celebrate my man A.K.'s birthday. He was relatively new to school and the chicks couldn't resist him. They fell for his fake bad boy image that they created for him. He was my dude though. We hit it off right away.

Max and I collected money for the beer. My motto always was it's better to have too much than not enough. Being that we were in high school, we weren't picky. You drank what was cheap. If you didn't like it, tough shit. This rule applied to the men, but women always had specialty orders. We had to get fruity drinks but if you want to party with chicks, it was a small price to pay.

The night started off calm. Just casually sitting around the fire. The Geek was the pyro. He would collect wood and throw anything he could get his hands on into the fire. We let him do his thing because without the fire, there was only moonlight.

When it was just the guys, the music would be heavy metal or something harder to make us feel tough, but as soon as the ladies showed up, that early 2000's pop music came on with the quickness. The girls that were a part of the crew were like family to me. They were all very kind and supportive. We were a very tight knit group of friends. We had each other's backs. They would call me "the vault" because they knew they could bring their secrets to me and I wouldn't say a word. They thought this was because I was a good friend, but really it was because I liked the gossip. I liked knowing other people had drama. It gave me a sense of normalcy.

We got down to business quick. There was no messing around and everyone was in the mood to get messed up. We were smashing beers. We even brought out the beer bong. We called him King Bong Bundy. It added an extra element of excitement to our parties. The beer bong was a good way to ensure the girls would get drunk and they couldn't fake drinking.

Everyone was having a blast. The fire was blazing, the drinks were flowing, and Christina Aguilera was explaining to me "What A Girl Wants" while I did my Genie In A Bottle dance. When we got drunk, we loved to do dumb things. We fed off each other and it was usually a battle to see who could out stupid the other. The first instance was when I challenged Hubb to a duel. We took the empty 12-pack boxes and placed them over our heads.

I exclaimed, "This man has besmirched my honor and I demand satisfaction." We both grabbed a stick out of the fire and with no remorse for each other's safety began swinging our swords. The goal was to see who could knock the box off the other person's head with burning logs. Nobody attempted to stop us but cheered as we hit each other repeatedly. The hits went back and forth until one of my swings hit the front of Hubb's box. Bits of ember flew off of my sword and into the eye hole of his box.

"Ffffuuuckkk!" he yelled out as he ripped his armour off of his head.

I was triumphant in battle. I, for the rest of the night, would be known as the "King of Beers" and as King I demanded everyone drink up!

As the night went on, we continued to drink and sing and argue over the dumbest things possible. Everything was perfect. That was until The Geek stood up. Wasted out of his mind, he poured the little bit of gasoline that was left on an old, dried up tree. Before anybody could tell him to stop, he lit it on fire. The flames rose all the way up the tree. They illuminated so much of the woods that were previously not visible. We screamed and cheered as that fire scorched that tree. Flames going up over fifty feet in the air. We all just stood there fascinated. It was a really beautiful sight to see.

Off in the distance, you could hear the sirens. Then, through the trees and past the bridge, you could see the flashing of blue and red.

"Oh fuck, it's the cops!" Western screamed out as they were heading towards us with their flashlights aimed in our directions.

We all started to run in the same general direction and followed closely behind whoever was in front until the light from the fire was no longer visible. Then it was every man and woman for themselves. We all got disbanded and headed in different directions. My friend Angie grabbed my hand and we just kept running. We ran through prickers and into trees and I fell a lot. We finally arrived at the area where we could see the freeway. We walked there and eventually made the two mile walk back to Western's house.

This night was very special to me. The most important people in my life were all there. We had the most fun possible. I wouldn't have changed a single thing about it. I was the happiest I had been in a long time. Things were really starting to go my way.

The following week, I had an MRI scheduled. My trips to the doctors had calmed down. They were becoming less frequent. I hated doing MRI's though. The first thing that sucked about them was just the fact that my big ass barely fit in the tube. The other problem was that I had built up a fear of being in them. My mind would race in there. Being in one of those was the closest I could come to feeling buried alive. I managed to get through it as I always did.

The next week I had to meet with Dr. Abelmen. I looked forward to seeing him. I figured every visit was one step closer to being done. I sat there playing with the tongue depressors when he walked into the room. His demeanor was off. He usually walked in and shook our hands. Dr. Abelmen always asked how we were doing. I knew something was off. He sat in that little doctor's chair that spun around.

He took a deep breath…. " Frank, I'm not going to sugarcoat this".... Oh fuck me, I had a million things run in and out of my head. He explained how he took the first tumor to Baltimore for that conference. Well, what they found out from the conference wasn't what I wanted to hear.

He said, "It turns out you have a very rare type of tumor. They are extremely aggressive and can pick and choose whether they want to be benign or malignant."

I asked what the difference was and I never asked doctors questions.

"In a nutshell, basically the tumor can decide if it wants to be cancerous or not. We have one more problem," he said. "There is a second tumor growing on the same side on your pectoral muscle."

The type of tumor I had is called a desmoid tumor and it derives from abnormal cell growth. It can present itself anywhere in the body where connective tissue, bone, muscle or ligament is present.

After that, I couldn't even focus on what he was saying. I started having a panic attack. All I could think about was how much I was going to be at the hospital. I thought it was like starting over again. I became queasy. I began to sweat. I can't go through this again. My thoughts became suicidal immediately. Just do it. You won't have to go through this.

After the moment passed, I was able to focus on what Dr. Abelmen was saying again. He wanted to start back up the chemotherapy. This time, he wanted to add seven weeks of radiation treatments.

"Why can't we just cut it out like we did the last one?" my mom asked with a puzzled look on her face.

Dr. Abelmen explained that we had to be very cautious.

"Now that there was another tumor and it was heading for the heart, we have to take baby steps in fighting this. If the tumor gets to the heart, things can go very badly and I love you too much to let anything happen to you," as he stood up and gave us both a hug.

"This is going to be tough. You're a tough kid. You have been through a lot and it's going to get harder before it gets easier. We're all fighting for you. Please feel free to ask questions. We got this," Dr. Abelmen said passionately.

From the moment we left the hospital, I don't think either one of us was able to say anything. My poor mother was stuck in this with me. I know she hated being there but she would do anything for me.

I looked at her with tears in my eyes and said "I'm so sorry. I fucking hate this." I felt powerless.

"We will get through this. I love you and you're going to be fine," she said holding back any type of emotions.

I was set to begin my first dose of chemotherapy again. Once again, I had to go to The Rainbow Babies section of the hospital to have this done. I was not excited to be there. As we took the elevator up to the sixth floor, I could feel my knees start to shake. I despised being in the hospital at this point.

As we entered the waiting room that was still more like a playground than a waiting room, there were two small children having a tea party. The little girl was wearing a crown and pretending to be the queen. The little boy was pouring her tea and was acting like her servant. It was kind of adorable to watch.

I looked over at the two sets of parents as they watched their children having the most fun they probably had in awhile. All four of them sat there with huge smiles on their faces, grinning from ear to ear. I couldn't imagine sitting there as my child slowly was dying of a terrible disease. I would often wish I could switch places with them. They would be so grateful to be in my position. This would make me feel incredibly guilty.

The queen walked over to me and demanded I wear the crown and become the king. I wasn't in the mood to entertain these kids, but I obliged anyway.

She scolded the servant.

"How dare you make the king wait for his tea," she said.

This made me chuckle.

"I'm sorry your majesty," he spat out as we all laughed.

"I'm Queen Colleen," she said.

I introduced myself as King Frank.

"King Frank, how is your tea?" she asked.

"It's the finest in the land, Queen," I replied.

Queen Colleen made me forget why I was there. That sweet little girl and her innocence made me totally forget that I was anxious, scared, and nervous. My only focus was on making sure the queen was happy. I played in there for about twenty minutes before the nurse called me into the back.

I took off my crown and was ready to hand it back to Queen Colleen when she exclaimed, "You are still the king and so you shall be treated like one" she demanded I keep on my crown.

"Yes, your majesty. I shall do as you wish."

I went back to the exam room, crown and all. I joked with the nurse about how sweet that little girl was. She said she was one of the most upbeat patients she's ever dealt with. She never stops smiling. I wished I felt like her but for that brief moment, I was free from thought. The hospital disappeared. The Queen, this tiny, little eight year old girl made everything go away. The chemo went successfully. I was very thankful to the Queen for making my day. That was hands down the happiest I had ever been while going to the hospital.

That weekend I decided, fuck it. I was so well-behaved the first time around. I did everything the doctors asked me to do. I was a model patient, but this time I was going to have a lot more fun. Max and I were hanging out at his house playing football on the dreamcast when his dad received a phone call from his work. Apparently, he was getting some type of raise. He was very excited!

"Boys it's a good day. Where I come from, when there's good news, we drink," he said as he grabbed a bottle of something and three shot glasses. We raised our glasses and toasted in his honor.

After that, I told Max that maybe we should grab a bottle. We should try drinking liquor instead of beer. Max agreed that sounded like a good idea. He said that his parents had a bottle sitting in the basement for as long as he could remember.

"Well fuck it. Let's drink it," he said, grabbing an old bottle of 80-proof Black Velvet Canadian Whiskey. Just taking a sniff of it, we knew we were in trouble.

"I can't drink this straight."

I asked Max if he had anything to mix it with. We both went upstairs to find that his alcoholic parents had nothing to drink, but booze and brews.

We hopped into my car to run to the convenient store. We were both excited to be taking our drinking to the next level. We had done plenty of shots but never really just drank liquor. We headed towards the coolers to make this critical decision.

"How about gatorade?" Max suggested. I shrugged off the idea. "Pepsi?" he said.

"Nah," I sighed.

Then I saw it, staring me right in the face.

"How about the ghetto tea?" I asked. This is what we called the half gallon of Dairymen's iced tea. It was a go-to drink in the neighborhood because it was cheap and delicious. We both grabbed one and headed back to Max's house.

Max and I, being the competitive people that we were, began to pour out the ghetto tea. We got to the halfway point. That won't make a strong drink. We need more booze and less tea. We kept pouring and pouring. We got to the bottom of our tea and there was probably just a little more than a cup of drink left.

"We might have gone too far" I said as we both eyed up our mistake.

We split the bottle in half. We poured the Black Velvet into our ghetto tea. We took a sip. The ghetto tea did absolutely nothing. That sip was straight Canadian Whiskey!

"Fuck that's potent," as I cringed from the taste of it.

Our eyes were watering. The next sip I took, I pinched my nose. This really diluted the taste. This technique made it much more tolerable. Max followed suit. Now, we were pinching our noses and chugging as much as possible before the taste hit us. We did this a couple times. In less than eight minutes, we had both polished off our half a bottle of whiskey.

We were feeling inebriated almost instantly. When we drank beer it usually took us a 6-pack before we would even start to feel it, but after eight minutes, we were good. The liquor made my face numb. I was unable to feel anything. I asked Max to slap me in the face for some unknown reason. He did and it did not hurt. I just laughed. He asked me to slap him and I did. He felt nothing as well. I'll be damned if we didn't slap and punch each other over twenty times in the face all while laughing the entire time.

Once that liquor kicked in, we were wasted. Two fat sloppy drunks.

"Let's go somewhere. I want to do something."

We grabbed a bunch of beers and got into the Geo Tracker.

We went cruisin and boozin! We just drove around slamming beers and rocking to some tunes. We liked to yell at people as we drove by them, especially when we were drunk.

We approached the downtown area of Euclid. Max had seen a woman riding one of those Rascal Motor Scooters for disabled people. I had been encouraging him to yell at people, but I assumed he knew someone like this was off limits. Max did not get the memo.

"Hey lady! Learn how to walk!" he screamed at her.

He immediately regretted yelling that out as we sat there staring at each other for a second. It sobered us up for a moment.

"I'm such an asshole," Max said.

"Uh yeah, no shit," as we busted out laughing hysterically.

I was way too drunk to be doing anything, let alone driving around. We continued to smash beers. I didn't care about anything. I liked the idea of being reckless. It made me feel normal. When I was wasted, there were no doctors there to tell me what to do.

Max came up with this great idea to go to this girl Slwhori's house. Her name was a combination of slut, whore, and Lori. We were to assume she got this name from the fact that she liked to be flirty with the boys. When we arrived at her house, I parked the car over her front lawn. Max and I stumbled out of the Geo Tracker. Max headed towards the bushes to take a piss while I went towards the front door. I balled my fist and began to beat on the door. I yelled for Slwhori to come out at the top of my lungs. I could barely stand up at this point. I looked over at Max, who was still going to the bathroom in the bushes.

"I gotta take a piss too."

Max replied, "Dude, the whole world is your bathroom. Just go."

I think that I forgot where I was and what I was doing. Before I even realized, I was pissing on Slwhori's front door. This was half a bottle of Black Velvet and about six beers worth all coming out at once. There was no aiming, I just let it rip. I was pissing everywhere. It felt like heaven. Max was right, the world is your bathroom.
While my body was overcome with this euphoric satisfaction, I heard a blood-curdling scream. Unbeknownst to me, I was pissing on Slwhori's mom.

"What the fuck!" she belted out as I was coming to the realization of what was happening.

I was pissing on her mom. There was piss flying into the house as she ran away screaming.

"Oh fuck. Run!" I shouted to Max as he ran towards the car.

This did not stop me from going to the bathroom. As I finished, I jumped down the three stairs leading from the front door. I felt like the world was moving in slow motion. It took me forever to get to the car. I finally got in and got the car started. We sped off driving over several lawns and taking out several bushes.

Liquor was awesome. It was like a magic potion that made me feel invincible. Beer made me want to party, but liquor made me feel on top of the world. We cruised around awhile continuing to do dumb shit. All it would take was for one cop to see us and I would have been fucked. My life would have been ruined. We got lucky that night.

Chapter 7 *The Queen*

I had another MRI scheduled to see if the tumor was finally starting to shrink from the chemotherapy. This one was at a local hospital unit so I didn't have to travel downtown. I brought AK and Hubb with me because I guess they were just that bored.

The thing I liked about this place was that it had a Nintendo 64. The selection of games wasn't anything special, but just like with NARC and the E-room, I had a game I had to beat. It was a snowmobile game. Honestly, it was pretty generic but I enjoyed it. Maybe because I was in a hospital and playing that was better than reading some old Reader's Digest. A.K. and I started to play. As with anything, I always wanted to win, no matter what it was. I smoked him. He made excuses about the controller, but we know he got destroyed.

As I was gloating in A.K.'s face, I saw a kid sitting across the room with his father. He was probably about ten years old. His face was a pale shade of white and he was bald from what I assumed was chemotherapy. I thought about how much it changed my day when her majesty Queen Colleen asked me to join her tea party.

I looked over and said, "Hey buddy, you want to play?"

He looked up to his dad for approval. His dad said he could play. He ran over to us. He was so happy. I could only imagine in that moment that he felt like I did when I was asked to join that little girl's tea party.

I played him in a race. I crashed into everything possible. I loved to talk trash and playing this kid was no exception. He was eating it up. He even started talking a little trash back. I let him win the race even though that went against everything I stood for.

Right after, I was called into the back room for my MRI. I was in there for an hour. I had all my usual phobias while being crammed in there. This time though, I was kind of proud of myself. I did a nice thing. When the MRI was over, I walked back out into the waiting room. A.K. and Hubb were still playing this kid in the game. I leaned in to see what was happening and Hubb was kicking the kid's ass in the game. No mercy. I told them I was done and that we could go after the race. I felt a hand on my shoulder. When I turned to see who it was, it was the kid's father. He leaned in close to me.

"I just want to say thank you. You and your buddies made my son's day," he said, as he managed to hold back his tears. "You guys made my son feel like a normal kid. I haven't seen him smile like that in a long time… Thank you," he said sticking his hand out for a handshake.

"No problem. I know how awful these places can be. I'm glad we could help," I said.

We said our goodbyes. The kid gave us all high fives.

"Next time I'm going to kick your butts!" he said to us.

As we walked out, the dad stared us all down and just mouthed the words, thank you. That was an amazing feeling. That small act of kindness had the ability to change that man and his kid's life only if for only a few hours. The whole time, all I could think about was Queen Colleen. How this eight year old, living in her own fantasy world, was now having an affect on not only my life, but it had spread to me helping others.

The chemotherapy treatments were weekly. Each week, I would walk into that waiting room, hoping the Queen and her parents were there. I wanted to thank them, like the man at the MRI thanked me. I knew how much joy that would bring them. Each week would pass and there was no sight of this family. I was beginning to feel way more comfortable in the waiting room. I would have casual conversations with parents. I was playing games with the kids. I would make them feel comfortable. On the inside, I fucking hated the place, but you would not have been able to tell. There was one nurse I was particularly fond of. Her name was Julie. She was sweet but also had a bit of sass to her. I would make a smart ass comment and she would be quick to fire one back at me. Plus, she was cool in my book because she guaranteed that she could find a vein in under three stabs everytime. The more and more I went to the doctor's office, the more that was actually becoming quite the achievement.

I was halfway through a treatment, when my mom decided that she wanted to go get a coffee and grab a bathroom break. She asked if I would like anything. I told her no thank you. The chemo made it impossible to think about food. I was never able to adjust to that smell of it. I found the stench to be putrid.

I waited for her to walk out of the room. I called Julie over. I asked her where the Queen had been. I didn't want to do this around my mom because I didn't want her to see me as weak I guess. I think she would have suspected that something was wrong if she knew how much that little girl's tea party meant to me.

Julie grabbed the little spinning chair and pulled up close to me. I was a veteran in the hospital business. Anytime a doctor sits in that chair to deliver news, it's always a bad thing.

She placed her hand on my knee.

"Frank, I'm sorry. The cancer got her. She passed away the week after you saw her," she said in a calm, reassuring voice. "We wanted to tell you, but we all saw this progress you were making here and you had a whole new positive attitude. We didn't want to see you get down."

That's when that feeling came back. When everything around me shut down. My mind went back to the dark thoughts. I would become paralyzed in my own mind. All I could think was...kill yourself. I was having visions of how I would do it. Where would I do it? These feelings of guilt would build up inside me. I made myself feel worthless. There was no stopping it. I would just have to wait for them to slowly go away.

My mom came back into the room. That snapped me back out of it. I had to keep my feelings hidden. If people knew this was how I thought, I would be locked up somewhere. I would be labeled. People would think I was going to kill myself just like my father. I wished there was something more that I could have done to help that family and their little girl. Her short existence left a huge impact on me.

Chapter 8 *The Monster in Me*

The suicidal thoughts were becoming more frequent. These mind attacks would happen all the time. They didn't care if I was having a bad day or the best day ever. They would seep into my mind and it would cripple my thoughts. I wasn't teaching myself how to cope with these thoughts. Unfortunately, I was learning how to keep them concealed. I considered myself the great pretender.

I could be in a room filled with people. I would be making each and every one of them laugh until it hurt but inside my head, I'd be wishing I was dead. It was crazy that this was happening, but it was becoming the norm for me.

I noticed that little things would make me incredibly angry. Certain noises would trigger this intense rage inside. If there was a person chewing with their mouth open, I couldn't stand it. I would either have to say something or walk away. The new Frank was becoming a different person on the inside. He was starting to scare me and the fact that no one could know about this made it much worse.

These random thoughts could occur anywhere and at any time. The worst though was when I would be alone with my thoughts. People were a great distraction. Solitude was a real nightmare. The biggest problem would be when I would lay down to go to sleep. I had to have the television on. That would help me to focus on something else, but that was only helpful sometimes. When it would get real bad, I could spend hours in bed just thinking the most negative thoughts possible. The thoughts were always directed towards myself. They weren't about harming other people or anything like that. They were always about me. I could think of an incident that happened a year ago, something so minor that was over and done with, but if it crept into my head, it would stop me from getting to sleep for several days.

I'd always heard people say the phrase that they had voices in their head. I also heard a voice, but it wasn't in my head. This voice sounded like it was in the room with me. This voice hated me with a passion. I created this monster that's sole purpose was to tear me down and berate me with insults. The worse the voices got, the more I started to lash out. That monster inside took over one day in the E-room.

This was your typical day at The Euclid High School. I was gathered at a table with a bunch of friends in the E-room. By now, I sat with the "cool kids". I say that loosely because if you were cool with me, you were cool in my book. There were four guys and four girls who sat at this table. The girls were all pretty. I have no idea why they wanted to sit at a table with me. It probably had something to do with the fact that AK sat there and they all had a thing for him but in my mind, they all wanted me. They wanted to run their fingers through my long chilli bowl cut hair as they fed me grapes.

I was in love with this beautiful girl with curly, dark hair, and eyes that glistened when she looked at you. Her name was Evie. In my opinion, she was hands down, the prettiest girl in our school. For the record, I fell in love with almost any girl that would talk to me and give me the time of day, even if they had zero interest. I loved to flirt and had a tendency to say some mildly sexual things on occasion. I thought of myself as a charmer. I loved having the ability to make a woman smile. Evie and I were inches away from each other. I was staring into her eyes and telling her how much I loved her. I was promising I would be the only man she ever needed. I would take her away from this world and buy her her own private island. I'd treat her like a Goddess. Obviously, it was over the top and I was playing with her, but she lit up like a Christmas tree. She bit her lip as she played along with it and it drove me nuts. I loved it!

"Hey fat shit, you got bigger tits than the girl," said that scumbag Donnie, the prick who choked me as a freshman. "With that haircut, you look like a fat lesbian. You ain't into girls, are you baby?" he said and he was the only one laughing about it.

This fucking guy. I swear the only time he came to school was to fuck with me and I didn't even know him. The new Frank wasn't about to take his shit though.

"Why don't you fuck off Donnie," I said.

You could see he was displeased that someone had actually had the balls to say something to him. He leaned in as close as possible. We were practically touching noses.

"Don't you know I'll fucking kill you. Remember last time, don't you?" he said in a real menacing tone.

Without skipping a beat and as stone cold as possible I replied, "This ain't fucking last time so back the fuck up."

Donnie stood straight up, almost in amazement.

There were probably over 300 kids in that E-room. There was total silence. Everyone's attention was glued to the situation that was occurring between us.

"You ain't even worth it. I'm not getting locked up again for your fat ass," he said.

You could see it in his eyes. He was shook. He wanted no part of me. He must have seen in my eyes that I was not the same kid I was two years ago when he embarrassed me in front of everyone. I couldn't believe that was all it took. Standing up for myself. He was defeated. All this fucking idiot had to do was walk away.

"Hope you like breastfeeding, baby girl," he said as he took his hand and caressed it across Evie's face.

She had a total look of disgust come across her face.

"Don't ever touch me," she said to him.

"Fuck you, you dumb bitch," he yelled at her.

That was it. All the pain and anger that I had built up had surfaced instantly. All the guilt, all the trauma. Something else came over me. This monster on the inside wanted to let itself out. Frank had shut down. Another force came over me. I jumped out of my seat and looked this asshole straight in his face. I extended my arms and pushed this asshole as hard as I could. He flew to the floor and slid a good ten feet. That ignited the E-room. Collectively, they all gasped and shouted out "ooooh".

Donnie was beyond pissed. When he got to his feet, he looked around to see everyone screaming at him. He just got manhandled in front of everyone. He could have let it go. He could have walked away. His pride took over him. He decided to run towards me. I'm not sure he thought this strategy out very well. He came running at full speed directly into my arms. Now, I'm a football player who works out almost everyday. I have about 100 pounds on the kid. What he was thinking was beyond me. I snatched this guy with both of my arms, lifting him up off his feet. He was practically over my head and I slammed him to the floor.

His eyes rolled back. You could hear him snoring. He was out. Fuck him, that's what he gets. My heart was racing. My adrenaline ran at full blast. I took one last shot and gave him a quick kick to the ribs before security intervened. They pulled me away from him. Once I was removed from the situation, Old Frank came back. I was able to think and process what just happened. I would never want to hurt someone intentionally. Being bigger than everyone growing up, I was always kind of soft because I didn't want to hurt kids.

In that instance though, I wanted him dead. I hoped he never got up. If there was no one around, I would have kept hitting him. I totally lost control of myself. There was no rationalizing with that other version of myself.

They took me to one of my unit principals. I explained what happened.

He said, "That kid is nothing but trouble. Hopefully he never comes back."

I couldn't believe it. That's it, I thought? There was no consequence for my actions? He took down my version of what happened and I was on my way back to my next class.

That was the last time I saw Donnie. I don't know if he got locked up for something or if he dropped out, but I never saw his face in that school again. I was glad. Who knows what would have happened if we crossed paths again.

The weather was nice. The sun was out. I was hanging out with my buds. Ritchie, The Geek and Hubba Bubba. We were always looking for something to do. We didn't like just sitting around or playing video games. We had to be doing something.

"Let's go to the mall," Ritchie said.

We all looked at each other for a second and said "Let's go!"

We hopped into Ritchie's car. Ritchie was the type of kid who would sweet talk your mother and then go through her panty drawer. My mom referred to him as the Eddie Haskell type. He was our wild card. He was probably the craziest one in the group. You mix his ADHD, with his recklessness, and you had a parent's worst nightmare. I loved him. I always wanted to see what he would do next. The mall that we went to was in Mentor. We had to go to this one because it had the most beautiful women. I could spend all day there and never spend a dime. I know it's cliche being a fat kid and all, but I really enjoyed the food court. All the girls would flock there.

One of the perks of having Ritchie was that he wasn't afraid to talk to any girl. You point them out and he was on it. He would just ramble, it was kind of awesome to watch. The best was when the girls would try to ignore him or treated him like a piece of shit. He didn't handle that well. He would try even harder. He liked a good challenge.

There was a very pretty girl with long blonde hair in a sundress.

"Go get her," I told him.

He walked over to the table with her and her friends. Immediately, you could tell she had zero interest. She was annoyed. She wanted him to leave.

Finally, she yelled out "Get away from me weirdo."

Most people would be embarrassed. Not Ritchie. He just walked back to the table and was cool as a cucumber.

"You guys wanna see something funny? Give me $5 dollars."

I didn't know what he was going to do, but I knew five dollars was a deal. Ritchie walked over to the pizza place. He waited in line and bought a slice of plain cheese pizza. He walked back over to the table.

"Dude, I didn't give you money to buy food," I said.

He laughed, "You'll see."

He ran to the bathroom and emerged several minutes later. He had the biggest grin on his face as he gave us a thumbs up. He walked over to that girl . We could hear him apologizing.

"I'm sorry, I think you're beautiful and I got carried away." he said sympathetically. "I bought you a slice of pizza to apologize. I hope you like extra SAUSAGE!" he yelled, as he opened the box containing a single slice of pizza and his erect penis.

The girl screamed out, as her and her friends ran away to get help. Ritchie was laughing hysterically as he ran towards the door to the outside of the mall.

"Meet me across the street!" he yelled, as he ran out the mall and into the parking lot.

I couldn't believe this crazy asshole did it. That was easily the best five dollars I ever spent. We calmly gathered up our stuff and headed for the door. We met Ritchie across the street. I don't know if I've seen a bigger look of excitement on a person's face. We all got into the car and headed for home. This guy was so proud of himself.

"She loved it!" he said.

He was being serious. He thought she enjoyed it. Who was I to rain on his parade.

He replayed every detail of what took place and the sequence of events. He went over what he did in the bathroom and what gave him the motivation to "stay up".

In the middle of his story, he says, "You want to know the best part?"

In unison we replied, "Yes!"

Ritchie reached into his front pocket, grabbed the five dollars I gave him and said, "I didn't even pay for the pizza."

While he turned to show us the five dollar bill he had, the traffic in front of us came to a standstill. We were barreling towards a bus that was completely stopped. Ritchie slammed on the brakes as hard as he could. We were forty feet from crashing into this truck going over 70 miles per hour. Not one person was fastened in with a seatbelt. I could hear them all screaming at the top of their lungs.

Ritchie turned the wheel and headed between the truck and the guardrail. Just from the looks of it, it seemed impossible to fit through there. Somehow Ritchie pulled it off. He drove between there. He eventually was able to stop the car.

"Oh fuck" and "We almost just died" filled the car over and over. I could see them all breathing heavy. They were frantically trying to collect themselves. They were all scared shitless.

Then there was me. I just experienced the same thing as them. We were all just inches away from death. A couple of inches either way and there's an accident with four dead teens. I didn't blink. I didn't get scared. I didn't react at all. My heart never raced. I was as calm as could be through the whole thing. I could see that I was about to die and there was this amazing sense of calmness all throughout my body. My mind and body were prepared for death. It was frightening to me that this was my reaction. I was not afraid to die. That was not normal. That's not how a human should react to that. There was definitely something wrong with me.

When I got home, I finally had the time to sit and reflect on what happened. I replayed that incident all night. I just couldn't understand how it was possible to not have any type of reaction towards death. In my mind, I was happy nothing had happened. I did not want my friends to get hurt, but I wished something would have happened to me. I never wanted to feel this way. It was becoming all that I knew though. The constant thoughts of self harm were getting worse. The feelings of hopelessness and worthlessness were only intensifying. When I was alone with myself I was constantly sad. I just wanted to escape these feelings. I just wanted it to stop!

Chapter 9 *The Great Pretender*

It was the weekend and luckily, my man Western was having a party. This is exactly what I needed. I needed to be around all my friends. This would help get my mind off of things.

As usual, Max and I were on the beer duties. In all honesty, I loved buying beer. It made me feel privileged. I also liked the challenge and getting rejected also was fun to me. Unfortunately by now, Mountain Lady was no longer around. I refused to go to that old asshole. We had a couple places that were hit or miss. This was okay if you were buying a 12-pack or a case, but when you had a big order for about ten different people, it became a giant pain in the ass.

We went to a local chain gas station. We needed a place with a wide selection due to the fact that girls are picky. God forbid they at least all agree on the same drink to make it easy, but nah, they all have to have different fruity, citrus beverages. Western, Max and I walked in; three teenage guys, with a grocery list of alcohol products. This seemed normal. Too bad gas stations don't have carts because that's what we needed. We all start grabbing boxes. Western is shouting out orders as Max and I start stacking them up. Jen wants this, Heather wants that.... And so on. Finally, we have a stockpile of cold frosty ones. It takes all three of us to carry it to the front of the store. This is when I started to get a little nervous. If she ID's me, I'm screwed. Not only would we have to start this whole process over, but she would remember the fat kid, with the chilli bowl.

I approach the counter with the attitude of not giving a fuck. I've been down this road a million times. I'm standing in the front. I have Max behind me, who looks like he could be of age, but Western was also standing there. I don't know why he didn't go outside. He looked like Quentin Tarrintino with Buddy Holly glasses on. Oh and he looked like he was 13. We go through the whole process of ringing everything up. I was even getting ready to pay her.

That's when she looked at Western and said, "Can I see your I.D please?"

Oh fuck me, I thought. Usually, I would just say, you got me and walk out of the store, but for some reason I reached into my wallet and handed it to her. She took it. She stared at it for a couple seconds. She had this really confused look on her face.

That's when she said, "1984...How old are you?"

I flashed my award-winning smile at her. I knew the ball was back in my court.

I replied, "I'm twenty-two Ma'am"

I could see the bewildered look on her face. Her nose flared, she closed one eye, and looked up. She was trying to do the math in her head.

Finally she said, " $107.65."

I handed her the money. As she got my change ready, Max and Western had grabbed most of it and ran to the car before she could change her mind.

We were all good to go. I was excited. Between football stuff and the constant doctors appointments, I was ready to let off some steam. Western's parties were great because they had all my favorite people. Plus, they weren't huge parties. They were more like social gatherings. We would party in his basement so it was more intimate. We could also be loud and when the alcohol kicks in, I tend to get loud.

The music was going and the drinks were flowing. I was having a blast; hitting on every girl I saw and talking to my buds.

We started playing drinking games. I was never the biggest fan of drinking games that involved cards. I feel like they would just usually turn into arguments and not much drinking would get done. I only played because the girls did. This would give me the chance to showcase my humor.

We started playing some game The Geek created. The design of the game was to get the girls to take their clothes off. I was all for it. The rules were confusing and I felt like he would change them as we kept drinking. The game was basically rigged in favor of the men. Unfortunately, even with the odds against them, they found a way to beat us. There's Ritchie, The Geek and I in our underwear and these girls are taking off shoes and socks. That was my cue to retire from the game.

I wandered off over to the area where Hubb, A.K., and Max were. They were in the laundry room doing beer bongs. This was more my style. I asked Max to "load her up", as I kneeled down to chug a beer.

"One beer? That's cute." Max said, as he poured two beers into the bong.

He kneeled down as A.K. held the bong up towards the ceiling. In a matter of seconds, Max had chugged both beers.

"Your turn pussy," he said and high-fived everyone standing in the room.

I matched Max's two beers with ease. We were both competitive drinkers and everyone was starting to watch us.

"Three beers please!" Max yelled out in a weird British accent.

Once again, with the calmness of a seasoned frat bro, he took them down. He felt the need again to remind me that if I could not do it, I was a pussy and I was no pussy.

I told A.K. to fill her up. He gladly obliged. I closed my eyes and drank the three beers as fast as I could. I will admit that Max could definitely drink them faster, but I finished my three beers.The combination of the beer and foam fills your stomach so fast. You become afraid to burp in fear that you will throw up. I figured we were done. Six beers just sitting in my stomach over the course of a couple minutes is rough.

That's when Max said, "Let's do it".

He wanted four beers. Four beers is all you could fit in the bong. Thank God. The thought of it curdled my stomach, but when it came to drinking, Max and I turned it into a competition. Max kneeled down, took a deep breath, screamed out, and began to slam it. As he neared towards the end, his eyes bulged out. Each swallow became harder than the last. He managed to do it. Spilling all the leftover foam onto the floor and beating his chest like a caveman.

My turn. The drinking was about pride at this point. AK filled the bong up. I was determined to finish these. I kneeled down and in what seemed like an eternity, managed to chug all four beers. I mimicked Max's celebration by screaming and high-fiving everyone. We gave each other a big drunken hug. This was a way to symbolize that we were done. No more challenging each other. On this night, we tied. We both continued to drink beer and probably at a faster rate than everyone else there.

The night progressed. I flirted. I showed off my one and only killer dance move. I had dumb arguments. I was definitely intoxicated and I loved it.

There was a loud banging on the door.

"Oh fuck, it's the cops," Western said, as he instructed everyone to shut up, and hide their beers.

"Max, if you don't get your fat ass out here, I'm coming in!" Max's mom was at the front door, drunk and angry.

By now Max was wasted. He had heard his mother screaming and this made him furious.

"I'm gonna go kill the bitch," he slurred out as he stumbled towards the stairs leading to the outside.

When Max was drunk like this, there was no telling what he would do and his actions would either get him grounded or locked up.

Max pushed his way through everyone. He was dead set on fighting with his mom. He was in no condition to have this argument. The only thing between his mother and him was me.

I didn't know what to do. I just knew he couldn't go outside. He tried pushing through me. That didn't work. He began to scream some pretty horrific things at his mom. Hopefully, the combination of the music and the distance to the door, she wasn't able to hear him. My only option was to stop him myself. I cocked back and punched him in his jaw. This was the only thing I could think of. Luckily for us, he was so wasted that he just passed out. We were able to guide him in the direction of this old van seat that Western had in his basement.

Western and I headed upstairs to calm his mother down. She explained that he had stolen money out of her purse. I personally don't think he did. She was always at the bar and either spent it or someone else stole it. We were able to eventually get her to leave. She was a stubborn Italian woman and it was not easy. Western could tell she was drunk and made up some story about his neighbor being a cop. That was good enough to scare her away.

When we got back downstairs, everyone shouted "Merry Christmas."

While we were upstairs, The Geek and A.K. had duct-taped Max to the chair. He was wrapped up in Christmas lights that flashed. They found an old Santa hat and beard. This was amazing. I had wished that Max's mom would have come down to see that. I would have lost it.

Shortly after, we were all sitting around. It was less of a party vibe and more of a chill atmosphere. That's when it hit me. That feeling took over again. There was no rhyme or reason to it. Moments ago, I was having a great night. All my friends were around. Here I am having these thoughts. It's crazy that I could be sitting in a room with people I loved and considered family and feel so isolated. The alcohol only intensified these feelings. The beer made my thoughts seem more realistic. How do you tell a group of teenagers at a party that you're feeling suicidal? They would think I was drunk and wanted attention.

Usually the feeling would go away. Eventually my head would clear up. Things would go back to what I considered normal. This wasn't the case. I couldn't shake this one. My body was getting very tense. I was becoming anxious. I figured if I just went outside, I'd be able to kick it. When I got outside, there were a couple people smoking cigarettes on the side of the house. They asked what I was doing. Having a mental breakdown. Thanks for asking, I thought to myself. I ended up saying that I had to run home to use the bathroom. If they wouldn't have been outside, I could have just hidden somewhere. Now, I basically forced myself into my car.

Western lived about a mile away. I could have just gone home, but I decided to cruise around. I considered myself a great drunk driver. I drove through the side streets, just trying to pass time until I could clear my head and resume partying. I turned the music up. I did some car dancing. I screamed at the top of my lungs…

I tried everything to get this entity I created out of my brain. If only for tonight. I would deal with it in the morning, not while I was out having fun.

While all this was taking place, I must have been oblivious to the rules of the road. I did a rolling stop through a stop sign, where you pull up and don't come to a complete stop, but you slow down and coast through. I did that all the time, but usually wasn't drunk and wasn't on the verge of a mental breakdown. Just my luck, a police car drove right past me headed in the opposite direction. It proceeded to bust a U-turn. The cop car was right behind me. Fuck, fuck, fuck was all I could think. How was I going to manage to get out of this? Why the fuck didn't I just go home? What the fuck do I do? I continued to drive. Obeying every stop sign. Using my turn signal. I was focused on the road. The cop continued to follow closely behind. I decided my best move would be to head towards the freeway. I was a quarter-mile away. I just needed to make it past a traffic light and make a left hand turn. I headed towards the on ramp. I could visibly notice that the officer was starting to distance himself from me. I sped up. I drove as fast as I could get the Geo Tracker to go. I got on the freeway and the cops continued to drive on the marginal.

"Ha ha!" I yelled out in victory as I evaded the police.

The whole time, the cop was behind me, I forgot about everything. My mind could only focus on not getting arrested, but as soon as I felt that freedom, that dark feeling came back with the quickness. Now I was incredibly drunk, driving 65mph on the freeway, and suicidal. This was a lethal combination. I started thinking I should just crash the car and end it. All the pain would just go away. I'd finally know peace.

Something came over me. I was no longer in control of my mind or body.

My foot pressed the pedal to the floor. The Tracker began to slowly go faster. 70, 75, 80, 85, 90 mph I reached. That was about as fast as that car would go. I was heading towards the off ramp. I was 100 feet from the guardrail.

Once again, I felt no fear. I was void of any type of feelings. This was it. That was all I could think.

"Goodbye," I whispered to myself.

My foot slammed down the brake as hard as humanly possible. Smoke burned from the tires. The car skidded down the ramp. The tracker was screeching and rumbling. The car finally came to a complete stop. I sat there blankly for a second. What made my foot hit the brake? I didn't remember thinking at any moment that I wanted to stop the car. I wanted to hit the guardrail. I wanted to be dead. There was a lot of evil inside my brain. That night, in that split second, the goodness inside of me took over and it saved my life. At this point, I really should have gone home, but I felt compelled to go back to Westerns's house. Maybe I thought people would think it was weird that I just disappeared. Maybe then I thought that they would ask questions. Either way, I went back.

I approached the house. The kid from before said "Man that was a long shit."

I looked at him and laughed and made some corny joke about being 10 pounds lighter. I went into the basement. Nobody even noticed I was gone. We continued to party as usual. Max was still in the chair passed out with Christmas lights on him. Only now, he had beer cans spread around him as if they were ornaments.

I was literally on the verge of killing myself. I was so close to being dead and not one person in the room had any clue. I had them all fooled. They had no reason to suspect a thing. I was down there drinking beers, making jokes, I truly was the Greatest Pretender.

Chapter 10 *The Good Doctor*

Today was the day I was set to start my first radiation treatment. The goal of radiation was to shrink the second tumor down more than the chemotherapy had done. I was going to be doing seven weeks straight and five treatments a week, Monday through Friday. I was disgusted by the fact that I would be in that hospital everyday. I grew to despise doctors. I hated nurses. I felt like they were just lying to me. I was never going to get better. This was my life. Eventually, one of these tumors would come back and the cancer would eat at me until there was nothing left. I wanted to die, but not like that. I wanted to go out on my own terms.

My mom and I hit the road. We hit the light before heading onto the freeway. There was a blue car that pulled up on the side of us. They had their music turned all the way up. The speakers were bumping. The person from the car starts screaming at me. I look to my right and who should it be but my old buddy Rodney. I had not seen him since my freshman year. He had moved suddenly that year and went to a different school. Rodney was so excited to see me and the feeling was mutual.

"I'm coming back to Euclid. I will see you soon. We're gonna tear things up our senior year baby! The gruesome twosome," he shouted as the light turned green. "See ya soon and hello Mrs. Negolfka," he yelled as we drove off in different directions.

"That was Rodney, right?" my mom asked, needing reassurance. "Oh, okay...I remember him. He was always so sweet. He would always say hello and ask how I was doing. Good kid," she said with a little smile.

I felt like right then I should have just told her everything that was happening inside my head. I should have let it all out. Maybe there would have been a way she could have helped. I wish I would have been alone in the car when I ran into Rodney. Maybe I would have said something to him. I wish I could have expressed to him how powerful that hug was when he grabbed me in that history class. That hug still meant more to me than anything in this world. I was so afraid of everything that day and with that one small act, he made me believe everything would be alright. That simple act of kindness. That brief moment in time that I'm sure he probably forgot about had almost brought me to tears in front of my mom.

I did what I did best. I tucked that shit in. All of it. I added it to the pile of shit that God was serving me. Nobody could know how I felt or what I was thinking. If that got out, I would be looked at like a psycho. I had too much of a good thing in my personal life. The juice wasn't worth the squeeze.

When I got to the radiation department of the hospital, I had this unique feeling of calmness. I think the fact that I almost said something brought me a piece of closure. Just acknowledging in my own head that there was a problem.

I joked with the doctors. I had small talk with the nurses. It was genuine. The real Frank had emerged. This happened a lot, but not inside a hospital. I was usually a grumpy, stubborn asshole. They explained how radiation was different from chemotherapy. The main difference was that I absolutely could not move during the treatments. Earlier, I had gotten a fake mole tattoo so they knew where to shoot the radiation. I thought that was pretty cool. They also built me a cast to prevent me from moving my arm. All I had to do was lay there. The procedure was pretty simple. Once everything was lined up and the doctors were ready to go, they would shoot radiation into me. I felt nothing and ten minutes later, it was over and I was on my way out of the door. This would be part of my everyday life for the next seven weeks. Drive downtown, find a place to park, walk through the giant hospital, sit in the waiting room, do the radiation, walk out the hospital, deal with rush hour, and finally get home. It was all very monotonous.

I'm a junior in high school. My day consisted of going to school, followed by the hospital. Then, I'd eat dinner and be ready for bed. With every visit, I would get more and more sickened by the thought of having to be there. I grew to despise everything about it. There were so many nights that I would be unable to sleep just thinking about how much detested that place. The actual treatment itself was not that bad at first. That was until the burning started. The prolonged exposure to radiation eventually begins to burn your skin. The burn developed on my neck and shoulder area. As each day passed, the burn began to get worse. The burn became so bad that I barely turned my head sideways. I would sit in class and be in tremendous amounts of pain. It was also in such a bad spot that my clothes would rub against it. This only added to the problem.

I couldn't do anything. Why the fuck did I have to go through this? I just wanted to have fun, play football, and party with my friends. This left me unable to do anything. My happiness was now just being able to take my shirt off and let the burn heal. By the end of the treatments, I had no mobility in moving my neck. If I moved it too much, the skin would stretch. That would feel like it was ripping. Plus, there was always this sensation that the burn itched. The only thing that would make that go away was to press down on the burn. Obviously, that caused more pain. There was no winning. Even after the treatments were finally over, I was told that the burning would get worse before it would get better. That was a very discouraging statement.

This left me virtually immobilized with my thoughts on a nightly basis. I already had enough problems being alone with my thoughts. This just made it unbearable. The entity that I created used this opportunity to annihilate me.

I knew these were my own thoughts and I was able to rationalize that. The more I would get mad at life or have a bad day, the more this thing would bully me. It fed off my negativity. I hated myself so much. There was no reason for it. I couldn't turn it off. I couldn't deal with it. This just ate at me all the time. The images that I would envision were getting more vivid. The thought of my father holding a sawed off shotgun to his chest and pulling the trigger replayed constantly. This voice would tell me how worthless I was. How I should just kill myself. How I didn't deserve to live. Everyone would be in a better place without me.

The big problem became that these thoughts were no longer contained to a couple minutes or just while I was alone in bed. They started to become the norm. These attacks were often. Every day, the version of myself changed more. While this was taking place, I was becoming even better at hiding it. I don't think there was one person who had an inkling of what I was going through. I could deflect anything simply by flashing my smile or doing something funny. I knew how to steer serious conversations away and change the subject without people realizing it. This was second nature for me.

After the burn healed and the radiation was over, it was time to do another MRI. This was to see if the radiation had worked and the tumor got smaller. Going through that shit for seven weeks and there's a possibility that nothing happened? That was horrifying.

When we met with Dr. Abelman, he said " I have good news and bad news."

I thought, hell at this point I will take some good news even if there's something bad attached to it.

"Hit me with the good news," I said optimistically.

"Well, the good news is that the tumor has shrunk," he said.

That was very reassuring to know that all that time and energy were not wasted. He explained that the combination of chemotherapy and radiation were successful. The treatments worked together and did what they were supposed to do. They would be able to operate. The surgery was now considered less dangerous.

In my mind, that was awesome. We could cut this fucker out and move on. Less bullshit doctor's appointments. I could focus a bit more on the things that I actually enjoyed.

"So what's the bad news?" I said.

I had taught myself to always expect the worst that way you can't be disappointed. I used this philosophy in almost every situation.

"Frank, I'm leaving this practice and my family and I are moving to Baltimore. I will no longer be your doctor," he said.

I could see that this made him distraught. I was built for situations like this.

"Hey! Congratulations! That's awesome," I said with a giant smile.

The reality was that Dr. Abelman was the only doctor that I actually trusted. He earned my respect. This man actually cared about me. I considered him a friend. He knew me. He knew my story and he wanted to help me get better.

My mom was in tears. She hugged him and thanked him for everything that he did to help out her baby.

"It was my pleasure," he said and I believed him.

He was just one of those rare doctors who actually seemed to care. For someone who spent as much time in hospitals dealing with these people as I did, I think I was a pretty good judge of character.

He went on to say that the new doctor was an expert in this field and rattled off a list of his credentials. I was not interested. He could be the nicest guy in the world, but he had no shot with me no matter what. I hated this guy before I ever even saw him.

Usually the doctor says goodbye and walks out of the room. Not Dr. Abelman. He continued to talk to us. He walked us out of his office. He just kept walking and talking. He walked us all the way to the elevator. I had never seen a doctor put that type of energy into a patient.

We were saying our final goodbyes. He gave my mom one last hug. She was a mess at this point. He stuck out his hand to give me a handshake.

"Put that thing away," I said, as I spread open my arms to receive a hug.

We laughed and hugged. We got on the elevator and pressed the button to go down.

"Can't wait to watch you play on Sundays," he said.

Hearing that comment and knowing it was the last thing he'd say to me...It all hit me hard. This was the only time I can remember where there was a chink in my armour. I never showed emotion and here I was, standing in the elevator as the doors were closing, two tears rolled out of my eyes and down my cheek.

I was very quick to hide this from my mom. I couldn't let her see me cry. Then I would have to explain things. I wasn't prepared for that. I pretended to cough. That would be my excuse if she saw the tears. She didn't though. I couldn't believe I let my guard down. I couldn't let that happen again.

I met with the new doctor several times after that. I wasn't even aware of his name. I barely spoke to the man and if I did, it was a mere yes or no response. Of course, this new doctor did not trust any of Dr. Abelmens advice. He sent me on a tour of the hospital. He wanted his own MRI's, x-rays, and cat-scans. They were so much fun the first time, I could only imagine that they would be all the better the second go round.

After a couple weeks of non-stop appointments, Dr. Dingus finally had all the information that he needed. We were set to do the surgery at the beginning of May. He explained that this one wouldn't be as severe as the first one. This was honestly the only time I paid attention to what he was saying. He went on to say that he would not need to remove as much muscle and would be able to separate the tumor rather easily.

The surgery was successful. Dr. Dingus was able to get it out. I only had to spend one night at the hospital. I could live with that. I would only do a minimal amount of crying and complaining then.

I was in a happier place. Both tumors were gone now. The MRI's showed that there were no new ones growing. There was a weight that had been lifted from me. This, once again, meant that I would have less doctor's appointments. That was a huge sense of relief.

The surgery took a little over a week to recover from. I was able to behave this time and didn't get into any fights. I was finally prepared to go back to living a somewhat normal life. The idea of that thrilled me.

Chapter 11 *The Comeback*

It was the summer before my senior year of high school. I wouldn't have to go to the doctors as much. At last, I would be able to focus on football and partying. The two things that brought me the most joy.

Over the summer, we "technically" weren't allowed to have organized football practices. That's all fine and dandy, but those coaches knew damn well who showed up and who didn't. Lets just say if you weren't there, you would be running until you vomited.

I was extremely excited about this football season. This was my time to shine. I had played two years of varsity already, but this was the year I was going to play with all my boys. These guys were all my friends. There was also the buzz that Rodney was coming back. That would make us real contenders.

We were a division 1 school. We played against some of the best teams in the state. We also played against a lot of Catholic schools that were able to recruit. We couldn't do that because we were a public school. I liked that aspect though; the thought of being the underdog. It was motivating that some other team was considered better than us and we had not even stepped foot out onto the field.

The last two years, I played on the varsity team. I was the right guard on the offensive line. My sophomore year, I played with all older kids who felt the need to blame me every time they fucked up. I also felt like I played very shitty that year. The coach was not very fond of me either. If I had a dollar for every time that man yelled, "God damnit Frank " at me, I'd have quite the fortune.

With that being said, we still made it to the playoffs. We ran into the powerhouse that was known as St. Ignatius. They were beastly. I had without a doubt my best game of the year against them. Everything clicked. My blocks were flawless. My technique was on point. We ended up losing that game by a touchdown.

Then, my junior year was a different story. Those seniors treated me like part of their family. My game had taken off onto a whole other level. My fundamentals were solid. My hands and feet worked in unison. I was starting to become a very dominant player.

We went 6-4 with that team. We were much better than our record dictated in my opinion. The problem was that we had a first year coach that cared more about his ego than the players on his field. But hey, at least he didn't refer to me as "God damnit."

We would have these awful morning practices three times a week. We would run miles around the track. We would run up and down the stadium stairs. Sprinting, jump roping, bear crawling...you name it, we did it. These practices were brutal, but I'll be damned if I didn't love it for some reason. Oh and when we were done with all of that and you were finally able to breathe, that's when it would be time to lift weights.

When I hit the weightroom, I had two different modes. One was determined, focused and dedicated to transforming my body and the other was lazy, unmotivated and would just make jokes the whole time. This was my senior year though. I knew I had to ditch the old bad habits I had picked up.

After the first surgery, I had to retrain the way I lifted weights. I altered workouts. I would use less on certain activities. I had been doing this for two years and knew my arm's limitations.

With the new surgery, I had to start that all over again. I would do bench presses with low weights and do a lot of reps. I had to take baby steps to get things where they needed to be. I noticed now though that my arm would get fatigued very quickly. So if I did an upper body exercise, I would do something leg-related after to give myself a chance to recover. I had the whole summer to figure out what worked and what didn't.

One of the mornings we spent going over plays. We weren't wearing equipment, but we would still go somewhat hard. This was a great way to learn plays, run audibles and work on technique.

We ran this simple run play. I would pull out and go to the other side and block the defensive end. I loved plays like this because I'd get a little running start before I got to hit someone.

My buddy Les was playing defensive end. He was a 6'3 half Black, half Asian kid from Jamaica. He was quite possibly the kindest person I had ever met. He was a real sweetheart.

So we run this play and I pull around. Les turned his shoulders towards me as I came zooming towards him.

Normally, I would have hit the shit out of him because in my opinion, that's how you learn on the field. I did not.

I simply grabbed him and said, "Hey Les, don't turn your shoulders."

He looked at me like I shit in his cereal.

"Shut the fuck up," he said.

I couldn't believe it. I knew this guy for five years. That was the first time I heard him swear, let alone be rude to someone. I couldn't even respond.

We huddled back up.

"Run that play back."

We ran the same play again. I was going to teach him a lesson. Nobody talks to me like that, especially not on the gridiron.

The play began. I took my first step towards Les. I was flying towards him. Wouldn't you know it, he turned his shoulders again. This was a no no for him at his position. This time, I popped him. I ran through him like he wasn't even there.

I stood over him in triumph. As I looked down on him, he was staring back up at me.

I screamed at him. "Don't turn your fucking shoulders!"

I gave him one of those big Frank smiles, stuck out my hand, and offered to help my friend up. Les still in a bit of pain smiled back

"I should probably stop turning my shoulders."

When he was able to get back up, we gave each other one of those quick football hugs and that was that.

This time, as I went back to the huddle, I was in a bit of pain. My arm and chest area hurt pretty bad. I just kept moving it around and stretching it. This was obviously some reaction to the surgery. I continued to practice and just dealt with it.

The pain lingered into the next practice. I talked to our trainer and coaches. I explained that it was excruciating pain. It didn't feel right and I couldn't get the pain to go away. The trainer advised me to just relax it. Don't over do anything. This is your body's way of saying you're doing too much.

While I was walking away, my coach said he wanted to speak to me in his office. I was genuinely excited. I figured he had some type of good news to tell me. I sat there, eager to hear what he had to say. He lit up a cigarette.

He looked me dead in my eyes and said, "You aren't going to be a pussy all season, are you?"

Who the fuck did this guy think he was? Pussy, I thought? I'm the toughest one out there. I've done nothing but play through pain. I came to practices after chemotherapy treatments. I did 100-yard bear crawls with a tumor on my bicep. Pussy? I wanted to murder this man. He wanted to question me on the only thing I was passionate about. It took every ounce of restraint not to grab that man by his throat and beat the living shit out of him.

"No coach," I said, with a cracking in my voice.

"You can leave now," he said, as I walked away demoralized.

He even had the audacity to mutter something under his breath as I walked out. I shouldn't have to, but now I needed to prove I was no pussy. I continued to do the morning practices. I also continued to lift weights. The pain did not go away. It would either get worse or be tolerable. I'd learned to live through it.

I did this for weeks. The more I pushed through, the more I realized how limited I was becoming. The pain had gotten to the point where I was unable to get in my stance because I couldn't hold myself up that long. The mobility in my arm was practically gone. All the things that I needed to be able to do were becoming less possible.

If I would have rested for a month, this would have just come back. This wasn't an injury. This wasn't just some pain that was going to go away. This was it. This was my reality now.

My football career was over.

All the blood and sweat that I spilled over the last five years was for nothing. The one thing that separated me from everyone else was taken away. The thing I loved most. The thing that had the ability to get me out of my head was gone. When I played, there was no trauma. No guilt. I didn't feel worthless. I wasn't suicidal on the field. That was my happy place and it no longer existed.

Chapter 12 *Teenage Wasteland*

It was the 4th of July weekend! I was the most depressed I had ever been. If anything was going to get me out of a funk, it was going to be blowing things up.

I came up with the idea of throwing a party at my cottage out in Geneva. It was a small cottage about forty minutes from Euclid. Out there, we could be loud and blow shit up without having to worry about any consequences. I wanted all my friends there. I needed to be around good people. I invited all the usuals.

Max and I came up with the idea of buying beer in advance for this one. We would take orders and stock up so we wouldn't have any problems. We put A.K. and The Geek on firework duties. Ritchie, Hubb and I were responsible for camping supplies.

We had a local K-mart that had introduced the self-checkout system. It helped that this place was a shit hole and going out of business. Ritchie would rip off tags and replace them with cheaper items. We had done this many times with small items. Get in and get out. This time, we wanted to go for the gusto.

We grabbed anything and everything we thought we would need. We had tents, chairs, and coolers. We filled up two carts and had our hands full. I would grab the item and Ritchie would do his magic. As we headed towards the "self scam" as we called it, we noticed there was a security guard.

"Well there goes that idea," Hubb said.

"Haha,' Ritchie blurted out. "Fuck that guy."

Ritchie saw this guy as a challenge and loved it. I looked at the guy and pictured myself doing community service when he caught us.

On the spot, Ritchie devised a plan. I was to pull the car around and park it right in front of the building by the discounted pop machine. Those pop machines that sold the generic pops like Mountain Dude, Dr. Popper, and Popsi Cola.

While I was gone, he told Hubb to go to the bathroom and make a mess. He wanted him to throw shit around, leave the water running, and just fuck it up a little. We reconvened in the back of the store. Hubbs' job was to distract the security guard and get him to go look at the bathroom. He was hesitant, but agreed.

Hubb walked up to the security guard. You could see from his demeanor that he was terrified.

"Dude! Ritchie. He can't even speak. Look how fucking nervous he is," I said.

Ritchie grinned, "I know, that's why we sent him," he said with a slightly evil snicker. "When he stutters, it will distract the guard and he will wanna help him. I guarantee it."

We were 40 feet away and you could hear this poor kid struggling to get the words out.

"Bbbaatttthhhroomm, mmeeessssss," as he pointed towards the bathroom he just messed up. The security guard put his arm around Hubb and escorted him to the bathroom.

"Lets go!" Ritchie instructed as we calmly walked out with both carts.

"We didn't scan them, you idiot."

We walked through the detectors without them making noise. This nut job was cackling the whole time. We threw everything into his car. I jumped into the passenger seat.

"Let's get the fuck out of here!" I yelled at him in one of those real quiet voices.

"You want a pop?" he asked, as he walked over to the pop machine to buy a Dr. Popper. He was crazy. He got off on situations like this.

We picked Hubb up down the street. Ritchie gave him the can of pop almost like a reward for a job done to perfection.

"How much was all this shit?" Hubb asked.

Ritchie didn't say a word and Hubb just knew what that meant.

"One question…How did you know the alarm wouldn't go off?" I asked.

"I was hoping you would ask that question," he said, on the edge of excitement. "Remember when I asked you to move the car?" he said giggling.

"Uh yeah," I uttered.

"Welllllll…," he said, as he removed a price tag from the back of my shirt. "I unplugged it as soon as we saw that guy, while you ding dongs were shopping. I had to see if it worked," he explained.

He used us both as bait. I had no clue. He was a mastermind. He thought of everything.

We were all set on supplies and beer. The Geek and A.K. were able to secure some fireworks and some American made explosives. We all met at Western's that morning. We double checked to make sure we had everything and we were on our way. Four cars loaded with free camping equipment, alcohol, fireworks and filled with rowdy teens, ready to celebrate America's independence.

The cottage was built on about three acres of land so there was plenty of room for stupid activities. There was only one rule. It was to use the cottage sparingly. Limit the amount of people going in and out.

The cottage had a way of bringing out a different side of people. Maybe because we were all city kids and being in the country was as close to any type of freedom we'd ever known. When we arrived, everyone had a chance to put up tents and get settled in. It was a very relaxed environment. We had tons of wood and it was The Geek's job to keep the fire going. I warned him that if he had another incident like at The Spot, I would beat his ass. He assured me he would behave to the best of his abilities.

We put Western in charge of the grill. For lunch, he kept it simple. We had hot dogs. Western's mom was nice enough to whip us up some sides to go with everything. She must have made two gallons of potato salad and sent all the condiments we would possibly need. She even threw in some sparklers. How sweet!

We all promised we would refrain from drinking too early. We didn't want to pass out too early. That did not take us long to abandon that theory. By noon, all the men had cracked open a cold frosty one and it was on. The girls were much more responsible. They all waited till later.

Within an hour, the cottage had gotten its first victim. The always mild-mannered, great guy, Micky. We played football together. He was soft spoken, but when he got comfortable around you, he would let loose a little bit.

The music was cranked all the way up. The Who's "Teenage Wasteland" blasted from the radio. There stood Micky, on one of those red picnic tables. He was just standing there nodding his head to the intro of the song. He was holding a tree branch that was about four feet long. He began mouthing the words to the song and using the branch as an air guitar. You would have thought he was a rockstar the way we were reacting. When he got to the slow part of the song, we thought he was done, but he just kept going.

"It's only teenage wasteland," he sang in a soft voice.

I don't know what came over him. I would assume it was too early for him to be drunk. When that song picked back up, he lost it. Micky started swinging his guitar around and smashing it against trees; screaming out the words to the song. He was using his guitar to destroy all the condiments that were on the table. Not one person was mad or upset. We all just cheered him on. We encouraged that type of behavior.

Not much later, I found him passed out in a wooded area. Max and I covered him from the sun and let him sleep it off. One man down and it wasn't even time for dinner.

The next one to drop wouldn't take much longer. This was my friend Angie's cousin. There was a rumbling from inside the cottage.

Heather opened the front door yelling out, "Frank, you might want to get in here."

Angie's cousin was in the bathroom. I could hear here heaving as soon as I opened the door. Just hearing that sound made me want to throw up. I was actually quite surprised by what I saw. She only managed to get a little bit on the floor. My friend Grace was able to get her the tiny garbage can that was in the bathroom before it could get worse. I was able to walk her outside. She had to have filled this thing halfway with vomit. I just wanted her away from the cottage and everything would be fine.

She was holding the garbage with both hands. I had my arm around her guiding her towards safety. The chorus to Bon Jovi's "Living On a Prayer" was just about to hit.

I raised my fist into the air. "OHHHH we're halfway there!" I sang along with everyone there.

In that brief moment I forgot Angie's cousin was next to me. I had let go of her to rock out. Angie's cousin began to fall backwards. I could see what was happening, but it was like everything was in slow motion. It was almost majestic seeing her slowly head towards the ground. She never let go of the garbage can. She fell straight onto her backside. The garbage can went with her. When she finally hit the ground, she had poured the contents of the garbage can onto her own face.

All that vomit was in her hair and covered her face. Little chucks of hot dog and potatoes were all over her. I couldn't stomach looking at her so I had to run away. I felt bad leaving her there on the ground, but I knew Angie would take care of her. If I stayed, I would have been next.

"ATTENTION everybody." Western yelled out. "I have good news and bad news. The bad news is...I forgot the cooler with all the food," he said, with a defeated tone to his voice.

"What's the good news?" Ritchie shouted out.

"The good news is I found this awesome 80's power hour CD!" he exclaimed, as he nodded his head like the CD would save the day.

Power hour was a drinking game where a random song would play for one minute and you have to drink an ounce of beer for every song. It doesn't sound like much but if done correctly, you technically drink five beers in an hour.

There was nothing we could do for food. Everything was closed. It was the 4th of July out in the country. We were fucked. Thank goodness we had Mrs. Western's world famous potato salad, some chips, a couple hot dogs and of course, sparklers. This just meant that everyone would be even more drunk.

So naturally, we went through the whole CD; drinking every step of the way. To be honest, it was a pretty good CD and I understood why he was excited to tell everyone about it.

"Let's blow some shit up!" The Geek cried out in an attempt to rally the troops together.

The Geek and A.K. had purchased twenty half sticks, which were basically a half a stick of dynamite. All the men ventured into the woods to see what kind of damage we could cause. The Geek began with taping the half sticks to trees. He would light it and we would all watch from the distance. They would explode leaving big holes in the trees.

"Big fucking whoop," Max said, as he snatched one of the sticks out of The Geek's hand. "Yall better run!" Max said, as he lit the wick and dropped the half stick on the ground.

We all screamed, as each of us headed in different directions. BOOM! The half stick exploded sending bits of grass and dirt flying through the woods.

The Geek was pissed. He was told to behave and here was Max trying to kill people. The Geek proceeded to light two at one time, tossing them into the air without much of a warning. Once again, everyone darted off into different directions.

BOOM!... But there was only one explosion this time. We all waited in anticipation for the other to go off. We all started to tiptoe nervously back towards each other.

"Fucking dud," The Geek said, as we started to approach the half stick that sat on the ground for almost a minute.

As soon as we all seemed to let our guard down...BOOM!!! The explosion hit really close to home this time. We were about twenty feet away. I felt shards of shrapnel and dirt graze my face. The blast made my ears ring, but once again, I was unphased by this. There was no emotion from me. My heart wasn't racing, I wasn't scared. I just stood there almost as if nothing happened.

I could see the fear and the disbelief on the faces of my friends. That shocked look, like they realized how lucky they were to still be standing there. I quickly emulated what I saw them doing. I made myself breathe heavy. I opened my eyes wide to give that look of horror. I played right along with the rest of them.

This time, my behavior didn't catch me off guard. I kind of expected to react like that in these situations now. I'd grown to accept the idea of death. It was not a fear of mine. I embraced the idea of it.

"I think that's enough of the half sticks for now," AK said, being the voice of reason.

We all concurred. Plus we still have actual fireworks to save for later.

By now, we were all boozing pretty good. Everyone was having a good time. The drinking games were going. James Bong Jr. made a special guest appearance for a little bit. It was a great distraction from all the bullshit that was happening in my world.

Night time was steadily approaching. The Geek was setting up all the fireworks. This was his time in the spotlight. He had to make sure everything was perfect. Everyone gathered around up front.

"Here ye, here ye," The Geek shouted out. "May you all rise for the singing of our National Anthem," he said, as everyone stood up and removed our hats. "I Pledge of Allegiance...," he sang out.

We all looked at each other confused, but smiling; even though it was the wrong song and I'm not sure if he did it trying to be funny or not. We all joined in and recited The Pledge of Allegiance with him.

I looked around at all my friends. They were all happy. As I sat there, I wondered if any of them were going through what I was going through. Did they have the same thoughts? Were they just as good of an actor as I was? How would I know?

I had given up on the idea that I would ever tell anybody what I was thinking. I had a couple opportunities and dropped the ball. I dreaded being alone with my thoughts, but even being around people and having fun couldn't prevent me from thinking like this.

The first firework shot up into the air. Red and blue bursts lit up the sky. Every single person had their head tilted upward staring at the show. I couldn't help but watch them. The happiness on all of their faces. That was all I wanted. I wanted to enjoy things like they did.

I really started to question myself. If I can't find happiness surrounded by friends, drinking and partying, would I ever feel normal? Would these thoughts go away?

While everyone there was distracted by fireworks, I was having an internal battle. Why did my father kill himself? Why does God hate me? Should I kill myself? What the fuck is wrong with me? I thought to myself. I hated myself for thinking like this. I hated feeling like this.

I felt like I was in a hole of depression. When I tried to get out, I just sunk deeper. There was no winning. I was spiraling downwards.That's when I decided I wanted to give up. I was done. I did not want to live anymore.

I was going to kill myself. I was going to do it soon.

The fireworks had ended. Everyone gathered back over by the fire. My body had a sense of relief now that I decided I was going to end my life. I went back to partying. I continued to drink. I made jokes. I was the life of the party.

One by one, everybody started to pass out, until I was the last one left. I sat there the whole rest of the night starting at the fire and listening to music by myself. On the outside, I assumed I appeared as calm as can be, but on the inside, my mind raced. My thoughts were so negative and consuming. If I would have had a gun, I would not have made it through the night.

The sun started to rise. The fire was just coals and smoke by now. The music was still on and I was still in that chair. I didn't even attempt to sleep. I knew it wouldn't be possible.

The first person up was Heather. She stumbled over towards me complaining of a headache and if she didn't eat something, she would die.

"Come on, let's go grab breakfast," I said.

We hopped into the tracker and found the nearest grocery store. We grabbed a ton of eggs, a couple loaves of bread and some sausage links.

When we got back, almost everyone was awake. The sight of food turned us into heroes.

"Oh God, thank you!" Angie said, looking like death that morning.

"Western, cook that shit up," I said.

While he cooked, we all started to clean up and put shit away. Angie's cousin approached me to say thank you for having her over. I could still see chunks in her hair. I once again became nauseous. I think she was oblivious to the fact that she poured her own vomit onto her face and I sure as shit wasn't telling her.

Everyone piled into a car and we headed back towards civilization.

The whole ride home I joked and laughed. There was no way anyone would have known that I was dead set on ending my life. That was how I wanted it.

Chapter 13 *Premeditated*

I found it kind of crazy, now that I had made this decision to end my life, I was in no hurry. I wasn't going back on it, but I also felt no need to rush it. I spent a lot of time thinking about it. Everywhere I went and everything that I did, it would pop into my brain, just to remind me that the day was coming. I wanted to see my friends a little bit more. I wanted to spend time with my family. I wanted to exit this world on a good note.

Once the decision was made, I envisioned every way possible of doing it. I had almost built my own set of rules for doing the deed.

Rule number one: My mom could not find the body. It was bad enough I was putting her in this situation again. I could not have the poor woman have that be her final image of me.

Rule number two: Absolutely no one could find out before I did it. The ball was rolling and the decision was set in stone.

Rule number three: Don't leave a mess. After my dad shot himself, you could still see blood in the carpet. There were bone fragments as well. That's traumatizing. No one needs to see that.

Rule number four: Do not leave a note.

Rule number five: No going back. This was the solution I had come up with to end my pain.

I thought endlessly of different ways to do it. I thought of almost every way possible. I would come up with an idea and then begin to weigh the pros and cons. There was the slitting of the wrists. I thought about it a lot, but I'm too squeamish and the sight of blood irks me. Plus, I didn't want to leave a big mess like that. That would break rule number three.

There was also the copycat method. I could get my hands on a shotgun and replicate the way my father went out. That would also break rule number three. Also, since I was going to do this, I figured I might as well bring my own uniqueness to the table.

The overdose of pills. At first, this was the way I thought it would truly end. The more I thought about it though, the more I realized that there was too much risk involved. What if I didn't take enough? What if I took the wrong thing and just ended up messed up and still alive?

I could jump off something. The only place I could think of doing that was The Spot. That's because it was in a secluded area, but I felt that the bridge just wasn't high enough to get the job done.

I could leave the car running in the garage. I'd always heard that was quick and painless. I couldn't do it at home. That would break rule number one. Then, all I could think about was my poor mother having to sit in the exact spot where her son died. That made me feel awful. That was no longer an option.

I could hang myself. That one quickly went out the window though. I was too hefty. What if the rope broke? Or my weight did some structural damage? There were too many questions on that one.

What about drowning? I could drown myself in the same lake where my father's ashes were spread. Then, it would seem like I was killing myself because I was depressed my dad shot himself. That just wasn't true. This was my own thing. These were my own problems.

These were just a few of the ways. The thought process never stopped. If I was using the toaster, I would think of throwing it in the bathtub. If I saw a cop, I would think of pulling a gun on him. Cars would make me think about jumping into traffic. It was never ending.

Then it hit me. I already had the perfect idea. I could kill myself and it would not violate any of my rules.

I decided I was going to get wasted and crash the tracker. It was genius. I could get what I wanted. I would no longer be alive. Plus, people would think it was just a terrible teenage drunk driving accident. It would be just like last time, but there would be no hitting the brakes.

Now that I knew how the story was going to end, I had to figure out when was the right time to do it. This was a bit trickier. I needed the right setting and the perfect scenario. I couldn't just do it after a casual night of drinking with a couple friends. One was because I didn't want them to feel guilty and two was because I knew I wanted to drink a shitload of alcohol when I finally did it. I needed a party.

The next couple weeks, I waited patiently for the opportunity to present itself. In the meantime, I figured I would do my best to be a great family member and friend.

There was that selfish piece of me that wanted people to miss me. I wasn't doing this for attention. I just wanted people to say I was a good guy and that I'd be missed. I wanted to leave behind the good piece of me. The kind, caring, gentle giant. The guy who would go out of his way to make other people happy, even though he couldn't figure out how to make himself happy.

I continued to go through the motions. I was still attending football practices. I figured if I couldn't be physically on the field, the least I could do was be there to support my guys. They were like family.

I was still going to doctor's appointments. I'll tell ya, if I was barely paying attention to them before, now I was full blown ignoring them. What are you gonna say? I have another tumor? Aww, geez! I only went because I did not want my mom to suspect anything. She was the only person who would have been capable of talking me out of it now.

There was one afternoon where a couple of us decided to go fishing. We had this nice little place down by the lake where we could fish off a pier. We liked it here because we could all relax, sit by each other and dip the old rod in the water.

There was a grizzled, old drunk asshole and his hillbilly biker wife, who ran the place. They were probably in their early fifties. They charged three dollars to fish there. They also had this little shitty concession stand that served burgers and hot dogs. The health department should have been notified about these gross monsters touching food that people were eating.

His name was Big John and his toothless partner in crime was Mrs. Vicky. Oh God, did we love to fuck with them. I wouldn't have condoned this behavior but they were the type of people who deserved it.

The Geek, Hubb, Ritchie and I had just gotten all of our stuff together, baited our hooks and it was just a matter of time before we were catching the big ones. We were using minnows that we had purchased from the bait shop down the street. We refused to buy Big John's shitty overpriced dead bait.

Less than five minutes into our day, Big John stumbles his drunk self over to us, holding some no name brand of beer in his hand. His face and beard were covered with chewing tobacco.

"You little queers don't know how to fish," as chew flew out of his mouth.

We were used to him talking like this. That's the only way he knew. It wasn't just us, it was everyone there. The only exception were his redneck hillbilly buddies. He was cool with them.

The Geek's line bent down with something fierce. Before he could reach down to grab his pole, Big John had grabbed it.

"What the fuck, you old drunk?" he said, as he went to grab the pole out of his hands.

Big John gave The Geek a slight shove. "Let a man show you how it's done," he yelled out with pride.

Before we knew it, the fish was gone and the line had snapped. He blamed The Geek's shitty line he was using, as he handed the rod back to him. That's when this old dick decided to kick over our styrofoam cooler that contained over five dozen minnows. The minnow poured out and almost all of them were gone. I wanted to punch him in the face. I wish I would have, but we all just yelled and screamed obscenities at him.

"I got the best minnows money can buy if ya'll need some bait," he said as he walked away feeling victorious.

The Geek was livid. I thought for sure he was going to take a swing. The problem was somehow this asshole was a respected member of the community. The cops wouldn't believe four kids from Euclid that came into Lake County. We would have been fucked and I'm sure Big John was the type to sue people and press charges.

The Geek and Hubb went to the store to get more minnow. This time, I had a plan to teach this asshole a lesson. I asked The Geek to grab a gallon of windshield wiper fluid. He gave me a confused look, but at this point in all of our friendships, we knew better than to ask questions.

While they were gone, our old buddy Mike showed up with his dad. They used to go down there a lot. They didn't fish; they just liked the view and would hang out. Mike's dad was strict so we knew we had to steer clear. If we would have gone down there talking the way we did and trying to fight Big John, his dad would have transferred him to a different school. So we just gave a wave down to them and kept our distance.

The Geek and Hubb came back a few minutes later.

"This better be good," said The Geek.

I assured him it would be, but we all needed to relax and get back to fishing for now. My line bent down. I grabbed it with the quickness to avoid another Big John catastrophe.

"Fish on," I yelled out, with a southern accent. I did this every time. Whatever was on the other end was putting up one hell of a fight. Inevitably the fish had lost its battle with world's greatest fisherman Frank Negolfka.

I had caught a pretty good-sized sheephead. These were considered a garbage fish that should just be thrown back. Not this time though.

"We're gonna keep this one in the cooler," I said in my best evil voice.

Mike came down to inspect the fish I had caught. We told him what Big John had done and he was gonna get his.

Mike laughed, "I can only imagine what you idiots are gonna do, just wait til my dad's gone," he said almost begging us. "We're leaving soon. I promise," he said.

"Not this weekend, but the weekend after, my Grandma will be out of town.
Party at her house if you guys are interested," he said.

We all said that we'd be there. Mike left about thirty minutes later.

It was time to teach Big John a lesson. I had designated everyone a job. This was very simple. Hubb and Ritchie were going to distract Big John by asking him dumbass questions like what was the best type of chewing tobacco? This would easily keep him interested. The Geek was to take the sheephead and toss it onto the roof of his camper/concession stand. Then, let that July sun cook that sucker. My job was to take the windshield wiper fluid and pour it into the big steel bathtub that he kept his minnows in. I thought it was only fair considering he killed ours.

Everything went off without a hitch. Ritchie and Hubb were stuck with him for a good fifteen minutes.

The Geek's face lit up with excitement. He told me that he was going to put it on the roof, but Big John and Mrs. Vicky were so distracted, he ran into the camper.

He said, "They have the nastiest fucking bed I'd ever seen, so I jammed the fish under it."

Neither one of us was able to contain our laughter. When the other two finally came back. They looked exhausted.

"He wouldn't shut the fuck up," Ritchie said, as he shook his head in frustration. "He just kept saying that Big Man Tobacco used to get him all types of pussy and I'm 95% sure we can all fuck Mrs.Vicky!"

The Geek and I just laughed at their misery.

"You Goddamn cock suckers!" Big John screamed out when he realized all of his minnows were now dead. He knew who did it. He slammed his can of beer to the ground and headed straight towards us. He had The Geek lined up in his sights. Three of his buddies followed closely behind him.

"I'm gonna kill you, you little shit." he shouted at The Geek.

We all stood up together. We weren't going to back down from this fucking guy.

"Fuck you and your hideous wife, you fish fucker," The Geek yelled at Big John.

Mrs. Vicky was quick to rush over to defend her own honor.

"You just wish you could have this you, little homo," she said, as she rubbed her hands over her breasts and hips. This instantly made us all cringe.

While we were distracted by Mrs. Vicky's beauty, Big John once again went for The Geek's fishing pole. This time, his intentions were to throw it in the water. He grabbed it and tried to hurl it out into Lake Erie. The Geek grabbed John's arm in an effort to stop him. Big John took The Geek by the back of the neck and slammed him onto the pavement.

This woke something up in me. I was beyond furious. I wanted to kill that man for putting his hands on my friend.

I grabbed Big John by his shirt with both hands.

"Touch my friend again and I will fucking end you," I said.

This wasn't an empty threat. I felt it. I had nothing to live for. This was the first time I was passionate about something in a long time.

"Fuck you and your boyfriend!" he said to me.

Without any hesitation, I cocked back and took a swing at Big John. I could feel the crunch. I could hear the cracking of his nose. This brought me a tremendous amount of joy. The blood spurted from his nose. He looked up at me from the ground, gushing blood. I could see nothing but fear in his eyes.

I wasn't done with him. I walked towards him determined to severely beat this man. I wanted to take out all my frustrations with life onto Big John. He was going to pay for the way I felt.

I was met by a wall of people. My three friends, plus his three friends were holding me back. I think they all saw what John saw and they were afraid that I would kill him.

That's when it hit me. I couldn't afford to get in trouble. That would derail my plans. I had let my friends see a different side of me. Hell, it was a side that I had never seen before. I was always the type to defend a friend or stick up for someone, but not to this level. That kind of scared me that I could be so violent.

I realized it was my time to go and the sooner I was gone, it would probably be better for everyone. That evil inside me was coming out. I couldn't let this happen again. Who knows who my next victim could be. I myself would never want to hurt someone that I cared about. I was lucky the rage came out on a piece of garbage like Big John.

We gathered all of our shit and got the hell outta there. Ritchie drove off like a bat out of hell. The Geek stuck his head out the window to take one more jab at the already defeated Big John.

"Big John sleeps with the fishes, fish fucker!" he screamed out the window as we left the old fishing spot for the last time.

They were all laughing. They were shocked that I did that to him.

"Dude, I thought you were gonna kill him," Hubb said.

"Nah, just wanted to put the fear of God into him," I said jokingly, but inside I wished I had done more to him.

In that car ride home, still stewing with anger, I decided that I was going to end it soon. I came to the conclusion that my last night on Earth would be at Mike's Grandma's house. It was time for me to go.

Chapter 14 *That Night*

The next week and a half, I did virtually nothing. I hid from the world. I did everything I could not to be seen. When people would call, I would make something up or pretend to be sick. I just wanted to be alone. My comfort was in solitude. I was one day away from the big day. I wasn't nervous. I wasn't ready to change my plans. There was a sense of tranquility.

I spent that day just cruising around. I drove back out to the cottage. I just wanted to see it one last time; breathe in that country air. I just walked around and soaked it all up. While I was out there I headed to the lake. I went to the spot where we threw my dad's ashes. It was by the marina where he used to take his boat out a lot. I sat on the rocks. I stared at that water for almost three hours. My mind was completely blank for that whole period of time.

There were no thoughts of suicide. I wasn't beating myself up for things I couldn't control. There was no guilty conscience. The evil voice was gone. I feel like he left me on purpose. He knew it was over and was letting me have this moment to myself. While I was there, I reached a state of nirvana.

Eventually, I was interrupted by a man walking his dog. He meant no harm; he was just looking for a little small talk. I appeased him for a couple minutes and the man and the dog were gone. When I went back to gazing at the lake, I could no longer stop my thoughts. They were back and as usual, they were negative. This time though, they were in the form of The Queen. She became relentless in her efforts to beat me down. I tried to reason with her, telling her to just let me be happy for today. Tomorrow you're in control, but like always, there was no controlling them. My efforts were useless.

The whole ride back was filled with violent, merciless thoughts. This sweet innocent girl had become filled with hate and vengeance. She refused to stop taunting me. I was tempted every second of that drive to just take the wheel and smash into something. That wouldn't make sense though. He just crashed his car into something? They would see right through that. I still wanted to make sure that NO ONE knew it was a suicide.

When I got home, I went straight to bed. The thoughts continued to consume me. The Queen had vanished by now. It was just me again. I could feel the tension and anger starting to take over my body. All I had to do was make it until tomorrow. That was it. This would stop. It would all be over.

The day was finally here. This would be my last day of having to pretend. After today, all the pain I had built up would be released. I was sickened by the fact that this brought me some type of delight.

It was a sunny and hot Saturday morning. I walked downstairs and greeted my mother with a good morning. We exchanged pleasantries and decided that breakfast sounded pretty good.

"We should go all out. Let's have a big breakfast," I suggested.

She agreed. We whipped up some eggs, sausage and french toast. I figured if prisoners get a last meal, why shouldn't I?

The food couldn't even bring me happiness. The overwhelming feeling of guilt made the food tasteless. My loving mother was about to lose her son. She didn't deserve this. My intentions were never to upset anyone, but to make my problems go away. The whole time we sat there eating, she kept asking questions about my future.

"Are you excited about school? Senior year!" She asked.

"Oh yeah, it's gonna be fun," I said, as I felt like a human piece of garbage for looking my mother in the face and telling her lie after lie, knowing damn well that there would be no future for me.

The more we talked, the easier the lies became. I was so good at pretending at this point. I don't think there was one person who could honestly say I had a problem. If they had an award for best performance by a depressed teenager, I was a lock.

I could no longer sit at home. I had to get out of the house and do something. I called up Max. I told him to grab a bottle of something and I'd be over in 20 minutes.

Now I knew I wanted this to look like an accident. I wanted people to think I was drunk and should not have been driving. What's the best way to do that? I planned on drinking more than I ever had. I was going to get annihilated!

When I got there, Max was standing in his driveway holding up a bottle of vodka.

"Hop on the party mobile!" I said, as he got into the car.

The bottle was only filled a little bit more than halfway, but I figured that was a good start. We grabbed a sports drink to mix with it and headed towards The Spot. We made our way over the bridge and through the woods. We mixed up our drinks and so it began.

"Cheers," Max said, as he hoisted up his bottle. We lit a little fire. We just sat there casually drinking. We had some great talks. We argued about movies, sports and girls. I almost lost sight of what this day was about for a bit.

Max was completely ignorant to the fact that this would be the last day he'd ever see me. I gave him no reason to suspect a thing. I never even hinted at the subject of anything being wrong.

We were there for about two hours. Mike had said we could all come over after 6:00 pm. The drinks were already gone. I suggested we go get beer and by the time we were done, we could just go to Mike's.

We left The Spot. That was the last time I'd walk over the bridge of death. We headed towards 185th street. That was on the other side of town. I took Euclid Avenue the whole way there to pass a little more time.

Instead of going to a place that would surely sell us beer, I wanted to go see the old war veteran. This was my ending and I was going to get that guy to sell me beer.

When we pulled into the gas station, Max was prepared to get out. I stuck my arm out to stop him.

"I got this one bud, my treat," I said.

This kind gesture should have instantly raised red flags. One, it was rare for me to buy somebody something out of the kindness of my heart and two, he should have realized this guy never sells me beer. He only sells it to Max.

I casually strolled into the store. The little bell dinged and I was on his radar immediately. I gave him one of those handgun gestures as I gave him a wink and clicked my cheek.

I proceeded to the back of the store. I grabbed two 24-packs of cold frosty ones from the walk in the refrigerator. I was prepared for some type of confrontation.
When I got to the front, he simply said, "Will that be all?"

I thought to myself, wow of all the times...today he decides to be nice.

He rang up the two items, spouted out some price and said, "Can I see your I.D sir?"

He had a real shit eating grin on his face. I was actually kind of proud of him. It was a well-played joke, too bad for him he picked the wrong day to try to be funny. I pretended to search through my pockets.

"Today sir, there are customers waiting," he said, but there was no one else in the store.

Fuck it! I pushed the rack containing gum and Black-N-Milds to the floor. I grabbed both 24-packs. I ran towards the door laughing at him; heckling him for trying to embarrass me.

"You son of a bitch!" He yelled out in disbelief that this took place.

He was still behind the counter. He had no chance of catching me.

"Fuck you. I'm sorry. Thank you for your service," I yelled to him, as I ran out of the store.

I jumped into the car. I was breathing heavy. We hightailed it out there before he could even get to the door.

Max asked, "you okay? You're out of breath."

I couldn't tell him that I just stole the beer. That we could never go back there. He would have been devastated.

I told him that when I was walking out, there was a wasp nest and the wasp started coming by my face.

"Oh fuck, I would have ran too," Max said.

He just believed it. That was the end of that. We were on our way to Mike's to get fucked up!

By the time we arrived, there was already a big group of people there. All my friends were there, plus some other kids from school that I knew, but didn't really hangout with.

From the moment we got there, everyone was in full party mode. This wasn't a casual sit back and socialize kind of night. Everyone was there to get messed up and have a good time.

I cracked open my first beer of the night. A free beer always tastes better, but a stolen beer on the last night of your life tastes heavenly. That first beer lasted about a minute. It was on! I was a machine. Within the first fifteen minutes, I had a 6-pack in me.

The world looks a lot different when you know you're going to die. You really do focus on the little things. It was like time slowed down for me and I was allowed to just soak everything up for a moment.

A.K. and Heather stood in a corner talking. I couldn't hear the conversation, but could just see the smiles on their faces as they both stood there laughing.

Western, The Geek and Hubb were in the middle of the living room, using the beer bong. All smiling, as Western struggled to take down his beer, causing him to spit it out. He got beer all over the floor. No one cared. They just high fived and hugged him. Laughing the whole time.

Ritchie sat quietly in the corner, his arm draped around some girl. She wasn't paying an ounce of attention to him, but that wasn't going to stop him. He was determined.

Max threw Angie over his shoulder. She was screaming to be put down. Max was beating his chest and grunting like he was King Kong.

This all made me smile. I knew at that point, my friends would be alright without me. They had each other. We were a great group of people. I was blessed to have these types of people in my life.

I wish I could have stayed in that moment a while longer. Seeing their happiness made me happy.

"I'll kill myself if we don't win," some kid yelled out while he was playing some card game.

That was it. Just hearing that phrase being uttered brought on a wave. I shutdown. I was unable to focus. That feeling of hopelessness took over. I was a slave to my own mind, but it's okay. That was going to end soon.

I had no clue how I would react this time. Would I have another anger attack when someone did something to piss me off? I decided I should distance myself from people for a while.

Mike's grandma had an indoor patio in the back of her house. I took my beer and went and sat in a wooden rocking chair outback. When I got back there, I had about 12 beers left in my case. I told myself I was just going to sit back there and drink every one of them. The beers were like an hourglass of my life. When they were all gone, my time was up.

There was a little radio on the table next to the chair. I turned it on and tuned into an all oldies station. I just started rocking in that chair and drinking.

The anger I felt slowly began to go away. I finally accepted what was going to take place. Once that happened, I started to reminisce. I thought about my dad and that day. I thought about all that time in the hospital. How much shit my mom went through for me. What life would be like if I was still able to play football? What if my dad walked out of the front door that day?

There were a lot of what ifs. I had a ton of unanswered questions.

Just then, a surprising figure walked out to the back. My old buddy Anthony. We were still friends but we just rolled with different crews now so we didn't hangout much.

"Hey, what's going on man?" he asked.

"Oh shit, Anthony. What's going on?" I said, as I stood up to give him one of those half hug, half handshake moves.

We sat there drinking a couple beers. We were both big sports fans so we talked and argued about that for a while. Then we started talking about things from when we were kids. I talked about that time he saved my life from that jerk kid down the street.

Anthony was the only person I knew that actually knew my dad. He'd played basketball with him. The only person my age that could put a name to the face.

"I miss him," I said, almost out of nowhere. "I wish I could have done something different that day."

"There's nothing you could have done to stop it Frank," he said. "I'm sorry for your loss. He was a good guy."

I teared up. It may have taken him three years, but he finally said what he wanted to say all those years ago.

"I appreciate it buddy, thanks," I said.

We both walked inside the house to take a shot together. All Mike's grandma had was an old bottle of dry gin.

Mike was walking around with the gin in a red cup, offering people to take sips. "What are you a Pussy?" I said to Mike. "Do shots!"

"Fuck you!" Mike said, as he handed me that cup. "Chug it, asshole."

I snatched the cup from Mike's hand. The cup was ¾ of the way full of straight gin. I took a deep breath in and proceeded to drink that whole cup of gin. It was not easy and I'm sure my face showed it, but I did it. Everybody saw me do it too. That was perfect. That gin would tell the story of this night.

My stomach was in knots for a couple minutes. I was pretty wasted, but still functioning. I headed back to my rocking chair. I reached my hand in the almost empty case. There were four beers left.

Now all I could focus on was the task at hand. I went over the route numerous times. I had it all planned out and it was almost time to execute my plan.

One by one, I drank each beer. That was it. I was down to my last one. The only choice I had left was whether to drink it fast or savor the taste. I drank the first half relatively fast, but then I decided to enjoy another couple of songs from the radio before I left.

The radio was playing commercials. The last beer was gone. That was that.

I rose up from the rocking chair, barely able to keep my balance. I began shaking my head back and forth and giving myself a couple smacks to the face in an attempt to sober myself up.

There were no goodbyes. I walked out the back door. I headed straight towards the tracker.

Fuck! I thought to myself. Why did I park in the driveway? Hubb's car was parked behind mine. I had to try to get him to move it.

I headed back into the house. Luckily for me, Hubb was standing right there. I signaled for him to walk over.

"What's up?" he asked.

I asked him to please move his car. Hubb seeing the state that I was in advised me that I probably shouldn't be driving anywhere. I calmly tried to reason with him. I told him I was fine and I'd take that long way home to avoid running into any police.

"Just pass out on the couch," he said.

I was no longer happy with this conversation. I was done with this. I began screaming at him to move his car.

I told him, "I'll fuck you up if you don't move it."

Obviously I was in no state to fight so I had to come up with a different idea to get him to move. I got into my car.

"If you don't move it, I'm gonna hit it!" I shouted at him, as I revved up the engine.

Hubb had no choice. He had to move his car. If he didn't, I was going to do what I needed to do to get out of that driveway. He pulled out and I was free to go.

The moment I put the car in reverse, Anthony came running up to the car. He was also trying to convince me that I should stay. The kid who once tried to hide to avoid having to talk to me was now doing everything he could to try to save me.

He was to the point that he was pleading with me to not drive. I could hear the words he was saying, but they had no effect on me. My mind was made up.

There was no use in me hiding my emotions anymore. Tears streaming down my face.

I said, "Thank you, Anthony, but I'm done... I'm going home."

I put the tracker in reverse and slammed on the gas. Driving over the lawn, bouncing off the curb, and hitting everything that I could.

This was actually it. I was free. There was nothing left to stop me. All the preparation was over. No more lying. No more hiding behind this mask. I was going to make the pain disappear.

The final destination was only a five minute drive. I just need to get off 200th street and onto the freeway. I pulled onto 200th street and turned the music all the way up and rolled the windows all the way down.

I swerved all over the road. There was no way I was going to be able to stay in one lane. The road was a complete blur. I was screaming at myself. I was trying to not only hype myself up, but to make sure I stayed awake long enough to get to where I was going.

The only thing stopping me from getting to the freeway was a red light at the intersection before the marginal. This may have been the longest red light in the history of red lights.

I sat there with my eyes glued to the light, waiting for it to change. During this time, the past couple years replayed in my head. I didn't think about anything negative. All the thoughts were about good times. The friendships I created; the fun times that I had. Through this fountain of tears spewing out of my eyes came this slight smile.

I didn't hate life. I hated the way life made me feel. I spent so much time focused on all the negative stuff that I never truthfully got to enjoy the positive things. I spent these past couple years just waiting for the next thing to go wrong. I had become so used to the disappointment that it was all that I knew.

The light changed to green.

I wiped the tears from my face. Gathered in a real deep breath and I proceeded towards the freeway.

That brief moment of happiness wasn't going to stop me from finishing the job. It did, however, give me this feeling of euphoria. There was an eerie calmness that had taken over my body.

I put my foot to the floor as I got onto the freeway. The car slowly accelerated to 60 mph. I took a glance in the rearview mirror. There were no other cars on the freeway. The destination was four miles away.

I was struggling to focus on the road. Keeping my eyes open was becoming increasingly harder as well.

"FUCK IT!" I screamed out at the top of my lungs, as I clutched onto the steering wheel with both hands. I eyed up the nearest guardrail. I turned the wheel as hard I could to the right.

Right before the tracker hit the guardrail, I noticed a set of hands holding onto the "Oh shit bar." All I could see were the hands. The arms were covered by what appeared to be some type of light brown robe.

Without hesitation, I stuck my arm out. I draped my body towards that side of the car to protect this person.

The tracker smashed into the guardrail, flipping up and over it. The car was hurled down a fifty foot embankment, rolling and flipping the metal, crushing in on all sides. The windshield was mangled. One of the tires had been ripped off. By the time the car reached the bottom of the hill, it was unrecognizable. The car was crushed in half. The sound of police and fire sirens rang out in the distance.

There I was. My body slumped over the steering wheel. I was motionless. All my worries and problems were gone.

That was the end of Frank Negolfka...

Chapter 15 *Rebirth*

"He's gone...I'm so sorry," the doctor said, as he put his arm around her to console her. "We tried everything. We just couldn't get the bleeding to stop," he explained.

The emergency room was packed with family and friends. They were all speechless. How could this happen to such a good kid?

They all hugged each other. Another group of people huddled in the corner saying prayers. Everyone in there was trying to wrap their minds around what took place. Each person struggling to think of the words to console one another. Nothing could bring them any sort of comfort. They had just lost someone they all loved. There was no coming back from that.

I gasped as I slowly began to regain consciousness. The hospital room was very bright and it took my eyes a moment to adjust. I initially thought I was in heaven.
I was unsuccessful in my attempt? What went wrong? How was I going to explain this? That anxiety took over. I began sweating all over. What was I going to say to my mom? Why am I still here? I think I asked myself every question you could possibly imagine. I never feared death, but at this moment, I was definitely afraid of life.

The first thing I saw was a police officer sitting at the foot of my bed. I thought to myself...that's strange. He told the nurse to tell the doctor I was awake.

When he walked into the room, I was scared to death. My mind and body were in no shape to make up a story. I couldn't remember the details. They would know I was lying.

"You're very fortunate to be alive," the doctor said.

I sure as fuck didn't feel that way. Little did he know that was the opposite of what was supposed to happen.

He began to explain to me that because I am a big guy and the car that I was in was so small, that when the car was flipping, I didn't get thrown around that much. I wish I would have known that was a thing before I tried to kill myself.

He grabbed the little chair and slid it over. Once again, I knew that something serious was coming.

"You see that officer over there?" He asked.

"Yes I do."

"Do you know why he's here?" he asked.

"No, sir. I don't," I replied.

He went on to tell me that the officer was there for two reasons. One, he was there because he pulled me out of the car. The second reason he was there was because I was on suicide watch.

"Suicide watch?" I asked, trying to pretend like the thought of that was just ridiculous.

Inside, I couldn't believe it. I was caught. I'd spent so much time and effort hiding this person.

The police officer spoke up, "Hey, Doc! Do you think I can have a moment with the kid?"

"Why? What for?" the doctor asked with a bit of an attitude.

"Just get the fuck out," the officer said, as I smiled.

He said what I always wished I had said to one of those assholes.

The doctor sulked out of the room. The officer walked over. He grabbed the little chair and slid right next to me on the side of the bed.

I'm fucked. That was all I remember thinking. What was going to happen? Was I in trouble?

He leaned in close. "Son, do you have any idea what just happened?" He asked me.

"I remember drinking with my friends and waking up here," I said. The look on his face let me know immediately he knew that I was lying.

"Well, I'm going to let you know what I saw from my perspective," he said. He would go on to explain what transpired.

"I was sitting in my car, watching for people speeding and the drunks who are out late at night. That's when I heard this loud crash. I could see your car flip over the guardrail and roll down the hill. It was horrific. I thought for sure whoever was in that car was dead. There was no doubt in my mind."

"I flipped on my lights and sirens. I called it in. I was there within 30 seconds," he said.

"Not only were you still alive, which astonished me, but you were walking around. You were crying and screaming at the car. I approached with extreme caution. I was honestly scared, one of the few times ever on this job," he explained.

He told me that I had no clue he was even there. He said he was shouting at me and I was oblivious. It was until he stood between me and the tracker then I finally noticed him.

"I should be dead! That was what you kept screaming. There was so much pain in your voice. You kept yelling...Oh my God, are they okay? Are they okay? Are they okay?" he said I was screaming at him frantically.

Just then it hit me.

"Oh fuck, are they okay?"

I thought to myself I killed someone. Who was in the car with me? I had this overwhelming sickness take over my body. I wanted to kill myself. I didn't want someone else to die.

"The only thing I remember was seeing those hands. Who was it? I did everything in my power to try to save them. I'm so sorry…," I said, as I was trembling. I was desperately seeking answers.

"Son, there was no one in the car with you. You were alone," the officer explained.

That wasn't possible. I saw someone in the car. I can picture the hands grabbing the dashboard. I know for a fact that I stuck my arm out. I tried to shield that person with my body right before I hit the guardrail.

The cop continued to tell me what else took place. I yelled and screamed some more. Then I blacked out. The ambulance came and brought me here.

The officer grabbed my hand.

"I don't know what made you feel like taking your life was your only option. It's not. Terrible things in life are temporary. Learn to embrace the good stuff and not to dwell on the negative things. It won't be easy, but it will be worth it," he said. He was choked up and struggled to get the words out. "When all the dust settles and you have a moment to yourself to reflect on this, I just want you to ask yourself one question Frank," he said.

I replied, "What's that?"

"What did you learn from this experience? Don't waste your chance to learn from this opportunity."

He went back to his chair. He watched me for the rest of the night. Soon after, I passed back out.

When I woke up in the morning, there was a new officer there. On the little table to the left of the bed was a folded up piece of paper with my name on it. The officer left a very touching note. He put his number in there and said if I needed anything, never to hesitate. That felt good knowing that someone cared. I thought to myself that was a nice gesture.

For as bad as the accident was, I was amazed how unscathed I was physically. I had a minor bump on my head. My left knee was swollen and I had some scratches on my forehead from broken glass.

Frankly, it felt like a miracle. As terrible as this was, I was as fine as can be, just some soreness.

When I finally was getting ready to leave the hospital, some doctors and nurses walked in. Apparently, once you try to take your own life, you have to go to a place called Laurelwood. They specialize in mental health issues. I wasn't going to argue. Maybe that was what I needed. What I was doing now didn't work.

I spent a couple days there. I figured I should take that cops advice and try to learn as much as possible from that situation. The first day I was there, I felt oddly comfortable for some reason. The people that were with me there were all pretty nice.

This was probably the first time I ever really opened up and just let shit out. That weight was being lifted. While I was there, I realized that the whole world has problems. Some may be bigger than others; it's all about how you deal with them.

All in all, it was a pretty good experience for me. I left and felt better about myself. I was going to try to change the way I was.

While I was there, I thought about that cop's question a lot. What did I learn? By the time I was ready to leave, the answer was pretty simple. I learned that I didn't want to die.

Chapter 16 *The Silent Sufferer*

One week later and I finally had arrived home. There was an odd tension between my mother and I. Neither of us really knew what to say. I wanted her to know that none of this was her fault. This was all me. I created my own problems. I chose a terrible way to deal with them.

That was the old Frank. Once I realized that suicide wasn't the solution, I wanted to try to fix myself. I was going to be more open. The hospital taught me some techniques for anxiety and meditation skills. I was going to change.

That first morning home, my mom knew the quickest way to my heart was to make a big breakfast. This time the food tasted amazing. The eggs were perfect, the bacon had that crispiness, but was also kind of soft. Just the way I liked it. Everything was perfect. This was just what I needed to clear my head.

After I ate, I passed out on the couch in the living room. My body was still a bit sore, but that was the only thing bothering me from the crash. All that excitement from the past week had really taken a toll on my sleep schedule.

I slept the whole day away. When I woke up, it was 6:30 in the evening. That was one of those real deep sleeps, when you wake up, you feel like you hibernated for the winter. That was what my body needed.

I was feeling good. There was a little extra pep in my step. I decided to go for a walk, just to get out of the house for a bit. Just walking around the neighborhood made me feel like a new person. The air smelled a bit sweeter. The sun had this beautiful gleam to it. Birds were chirping and that would usually drive me nuts, but today it just made me smile.

When I arrived home, I had the courage to have a conversation with my mom. I held a lot of stuff back, but this was the first time I really opened up about anything. I told her how these were my problems. That they could have gone away if I would have addressed them instead of letting everything build up. I told her almost all of the details from the accident. That was a great feeling being able to get everything off of my chest.

The rest of the night, I just sat around watching TV. I was still afraid to see my friends. I didn't even want people to know I was home. I didn't want to have to explain myself to them. I was not prepared for that.

While I was channel surfing, I came across an old looking religious channel. There was some outdated looking show about Jesus. It was incredibly cheesy. I have no idea what compelled me to leave it on for more than two seconds, but I did. After about 30 seconds, Jesus walked into the scene.

He was talking to a group of people. He went to pick up something off of a wooden table. The camera did a close up of his hands. When I saw that, my whole body got the chills. I had goosebumps. I was in an almost state of shock from what I saw.

The same exact hands that I saw in the tracker that night were on this fake Jesus. They were in the same position. He had that light brown robe covering the arms. What I saw on the TV was exactly what I had seen that night.

I sprung up from the couch to explain to my mom that the image on the TV was what was with me that night. My hands were shaking. My voice was trembling. The hands were identical to what I had seen.

I was never really the religious type. I always believed there was a God. I just had a problem with organized religion. My dad had to burn in hell because of a choice he made. That never sat right with me. He wasn't a bad person. He just made a bad decision. Why should he be punished for eternity? He suffered enough while he was here.

Now, I had doubts about everything. This blew my mind. Was this some type of religious phenomenon? Did I have some kind of supernatural experience? Was Jesus in the car with me? By leaning over and attempting to save him, did that save my life? What was the meaning of this?

Then, there was the other piece of me that had to rationalize everything. Was I knocked unconscious? Was it a dream? Did my mind create this while I was passed out? The list goes on.

That night, when it happened, it felt incredibly real. When the officer told me what happened and I had concern for the other passenger, it felt real. When I saw this on the TV, to me it just verified that something magical took place that night. There was someone looking out for me in the car that night.

I felt blessed. I felt like God had a purpose for me. This sign was going to be the reason that I turned my life around.

There was one thing I learned about my life though. What goes up, will always come down. In this case, it did not take long. Within 20 minutes of having this spiritual awakening, I would receive news that would absolutely devastate me.

While flipping through the channels, my mom asked if I could turn on the 11:00 a.m. news. She wanted to catch the weather. Normally, she would be in bed by now, but I think she stayed up just to make sure I was okay and didn't do anything stupid.

The news came on. The anchors started the show by joking around with each other. All was well. That was until the male hosts voice dropped to deliver somber news.

"Cleveland teen gunned down."

In the top right corner of the screen was a picture of my friend.

The news anchor went on to explain what happened.

"The victim and his girlfriend were sitting in his car. They were wrapping up the end of their date night. That's when a gunman ran up to the car holding two guns. He demanded that the couple get out of the car. He then instructed them to lay on the ground. The gunman told them to empty their pocket and hand over all of their valuables. The victim told the gunman he didn't have any money. The gunman attempted to get the keys from the victim. That is when a tussle ensued. The gunman was able to free himself. He reached for his gun and shot the victim in the chest. The suspect took the victim's vehicle and fled the scene of the crime. The suspect is a black male in his early twenties. The suspect is around 5'9 and weighs around 165 lbs. The suspect was wearing a gray hooded sweater and black knee length shorts. If you have any details involving this case please contact the Cleveland Police Homicide Unit."

My heart sank deep into my chest. I was dumbfounded. Those feelings of joy and enlightenment didn't last long. Now I was shaking for a different reason.

That seventeen year old Cleveland teen was my friend Rodney. He was executed in the middle of the street. That kid deserved so much more than that.

He was the only person in a school of over 2,300 students and adults to come up to me and acknowledge that my dad died. His hug and kind words did more for me than any doctor or pills could have done. He was one of a kind. His life was just beginning.

Those old familiar feelings began to creep up on me. I was filled with so much anger. The guilt was starting to build up as well. Why would God let me live? Why would he take this innocent soul from us?

Here I was, doing everything in my power to take my own life and this poor kid gets shot for being in the wrong place at the wrong time. I would do anything to have switched places with him. He deserved to be alive. The world needed more people like him. People with genuinely good intentions.

I'd like to say that this opened my eyes and made me evolve into a better person. I wish that was true. The problem is, I reverted directly back to my old self. I never even gave myself a chance to fix things. I went back to hiding who I really was. I tucked everything in. I put on that fake smile and went back to tricking the world.

Epilogue: The Beginning

Twenty years later and sadly, there was not a lot that changed about me in that time. I was still depressed. I still rejected the idea of opening up about who I was. The suicidal thoughts never let up, but after that night, I managed to not let them take me back down that path again.

I walked through life without regard for the future. I lived day by day. I was extremely overweight. I smoked a pack of cigarettes a day since I was 18 and I drank like fish almost every weekend. I was just going through the motions without a care in the world.

That was until one night, when serendipity walked into the bar that I always went to. She took the form of a beautiful, blonde-haired woman with glasses and a smile that pierced through me.

I was instantly infatuated. Everything she did was adorable to me. We spent the rest of the night talking and getting to know each other.

We started hanging out more and more. When she was around, I was at peace. She had this ability to make me aspire to be a better person. Being with her made me realize that I wanted more out of life.

There was this new version of me developing. I started to regain a sense of purpose. I wanted to take on the world.

As quickly as she stumbled into my life, she was gone. I was alone again. I was heartbroken.

That voice inside me made sure it took full advantage of me. I beat myself up so badly. I spent the next two days alone with myself. I was consumed with suicidal thoughts. The more I tried to silence it, the stronger it grew. I was having a complete and total meltdown.

Life had given me that taste of happiness and here I was, dragging myself back into the darkness. I was at a crossroads. There were only two options at this point.

Option one: I could end my life right now. The pain would stop. The thoughts would stop. My feelings of guilt and insecurities would stop. Everything would just cease to exist.

Option two: I could address all these problems and start fucking fixing them. I am glad to say that I went with option two.

Why not see a therapist? I tried that once after my first attempt. The overall experience was terrible. The therapist seemed uninterested and eager to feed me pills. My dad took Prozac and that didn't end well for him. So to me, that wasn't an option.

I had to recognize what was wrong. These are my thoughts. This is my brain. I just have to retrain myself to think and react differently.

I grabbed a pair of headphones and started walking. This quickly became a form of therapy for me. I began listening to motivational speeches while walking through the neighborhood. I injected as much positive thinking into my brain as possible.

I also had to find ways to get myself out of my head. I taught myself how to meditate. Calming my mind and body. Focusing solely on my breathing. This gave me the feeling of extreme relaxation.

In the process, I was also able to quit smoking. I was slowly starting to feel the positive effects it was having on my body. That became one less burden to deal with. Slowly but surely, I was getting myself on the right track. The next step had to be confronting my past. This was the only way I would be able to move forward.

As I got older and more time passed from my father's death, I realized that I couldn't blame him for what he'd done. I traveled down a similar road. I know what it's like to feel hopeless and see no other option. I've always wondered if we had the same thought process. Was this hereditary or something I learned myself? I wasted so much time asking the wrong questions. I tried to hide from the fact that his death was part of my reality. I hope that he found the peace in death, that he could not find in life.

Unfortunately, when it came to Rodney, his murder was never solved. To this day, it remains another Cleveland cold case. I spent a lot of time and energy beating myself up over my friend's death. Wishing we could somehow trade places. That he deserved to be here and I didn't. That's not how life works. I know my friend is looking down on me. The last thing he would want was for me to feel bad about the situation. He was just too good of a person for that. Hopefully, we can find justice for my friend so that one day he may rest peacefully.

I find it kind of sad that it took me this long into life to finally start thinking about the future. Oddly, it's like a brand new feeling. I find myself excited about the prospects ahead of me.

While I was working with a guy, he began talking one day. He was telling me all his goals and aspirations. He had his whole life planned out. I admired that. I wanted to emulate his philosophy on life.

He told me a story about how he saw a homeless man with no shoes. He ran home to get some shoes, socks and a plate of food. He sat down with this man and they talked. The homeless man explained that he lost his job and just wasn't able to get his life back on track. My buddy bought him a motel room for the night and gave him a couple bucks to help him find his way.

He said, "Frank, do something like that and you'll begin to look at the world differently."

That story hit me on a different level. I became enamored with the idea of helping people. But who? I was too broke to go around buying stuff for everyone. The next couple of days, whenever I had free time, I would try to come up with ideas.

Then it hit me. It was all so clear. I should help people like me. The people with depression, anxiety. People who are battling with themselves on a daily basis. People who don't know where to turn to, but go about their day with a smile on their face.

It was December 13, 2019. Exactly twenty-one years after my father shot himself, I started The Silent Suffers. It's a Facebook group that I'm extremely proud of. The people in it have been amazing. It's a place where people can get something off their chest or offer suggestions to problems stemming from mental health issues.

While trying to create awareness for the group, I was sending out emails to celebrities, musicians and news channels. I figured if I could find one person to help spread the word, I could make a difference.

Within minutes of sending an email, my cell phone rang. The number was unknown so I didn't answer it. They left a voicemail saying that they were from News Channel 5 in Cleveland and wanted to do a segment about me and my story. After some encouraging words from my good friend Heather, I said fuck it.   What do I have to lose! Here I was, this guy who waited twenty years to finally speak up and I was doing it in front of a TV crew for all of northeast Ohio to see.

That was the scariest thing I have ever done, but also the most rewarding. That interview introduced me to people from all over. Some people just wanted to say thank you. Some just wanted advice and others reached out just hoping I would listen.

The world is a hectic place. We need to learn to talk less and listen more. We have to find a way to make it comfortable to have those conversations about things that frighten us. We all have a friend or family member that is going through something internally that is destroying them. Pay close attention to the people who worry about everyone and neglect themselves. The ones who want to make the whole room laugh. The ones who are afraid to speak up and the ones who won't shut up.

Depression comes after everyone. It's not worried about race, religion, age, or sex. It builds up and consumes you. You don't just wake up one day and have it. It grows in you. It feasts on the bad days and reminds you it still exists on good days. The dark days are inevitable. We just need to learn how to be better equipped to handle them.

I'm nowhere near close to where I want to be in life. I'm still lost and confused as I'll ever be. One of these days it'll all come together and the stars will align. The good thing is… this is just the beginning.

Made in the USA
Monee, IL
16 November 2020